For Jessica

Man with

No

Name

Part One

The Night Birds

Nanashi dreamed he lay upon a reed mat in a strange place, dreaming of flying through darkness. Wind pushed in against the walls; it masked the cries of night birds. People had come with him, although he couldn't remember who. Childhood friends, business associates, it was unclear. He woke within the dream to splashing, the gurgle of water through pipes, and sat upright, convulsed with fear. The others were gone. He walked from the room and along a narrow corridor lit by a yellow glow. A breeze ruffled paper streamers and caught his vaporous breath. He was naked and he carried a revolver in his left hand.

At the end of the hallway was an arch, and through the arch the air dimmed from yellow to an undersea green. The splashing grew loud. He crossed over into a chamber hewn from rock. The chamber oozed steam -- the steam wormed its way into his nose and tasted of copper and smog. Condensation dripped from the rugged ceiling into a large, deep pool. Paper lanterns bobbed on the water. This was an old and sacred place.

An attractive foreign woman, pale and blonde, stood in the way. Her kimono glowed silver and blue and white as the light shifted. Her blue and black flecked eyes were not downcast; they focused sharply upon Nanashi's face. Her lips were painted red or black. She shook her head once in warning and stepped aside, was absorbed by the shadows of the cave.

A thick, powerful man squatted at the edge of the pool, his hairy back to Nanashi. His shoulders bunched and flexed, deformed in their pronounced development, and Nanashi thought for a moment of a washerwoman he'd seen at a riverbank, patiently wringing her laundry. Clothes had been flung everywhere, cast off with apparent abandon. He recognized the fancy jackets and designer shoes. They belonged to his brothers in arms, the members of his clan.

The man began to whistle. His position concealed his work, but there was no mistaking the fact he gripped someone's jittering ankle, inverting it above the water while pressing down with his opposite hand. The splashing and thrashing weakened. Nanashi swung his head to the left, and saw then a sodden white mound of disjointed limbs, still quivering. He raised the pistol with impossible slowness, as though gravity had tripled.

The man looked over his shoulder. His face was the Devil's. "You're awake."

Nanashi pulled the trigger again and again. Impotent sparks shot from the barrel. The revolver didn't kick; it made no sound. Of course it had no effect.

* * *

Nanashi never made it home from closing down the disco with clan brothers Amida and Haru. He wasn't drinking anything stronger than coffee; his chore for the evening being that of watchdog and shepherd to his comrades. A waiter hurried to their table and informed them of a call, carefully ignoring the unconscious party girls, the wasteland of overturned bottles and shot glasses. Nanashi made his way to the house phone. Older Brother Koma was on the other end. He said they were to meet at The Palace of the Sunfish in an hour. He hung up.

"Screw him," said Amida upon hearing of the summons. He spoke without opening his eyes.

"I need another drink. Nanashi, ask the guy to bring me a beer, okay?" Haru slumped on a couch, a snoring girl in a wrinkled dress flopped across his chest. Haru did not sound as if he needed another beer.

Nanashi wanted to call Yuki, but was afraid to wake her. She worked the nightshift as a cocktail waitress at another club. He imagined her fumbling around the apartment, sluggish with exhaustion, leaving a trail of shoes, hose, her skirt and panties hanging from a chair; he saw her through the frosted glass of the shower, lathering herself, then in bed, damp hair over her cheek as daylight crept through the blinds. She slept naked.

He sighed and herded his associates out of the club, ignoring their clamoring and protestations. Long ago, Nanashi learned to "do as Family say." It was that simple. He'd only argued against the wisdom of his elders once. They made Nanashi chop off his little finger at the second knuckle as a reminder. *One down, one to go*, joked Uncle Kojima. He had kept Nanashi's pinky in a jar of formaldehyde with those of other transgressors. A floating white garden.

And as for Nanashi, the boys hustled him across town to Doctor Yee's office and had him fitted for a nice, snug prosthetic. He tapped his fake pinky against the rim of his glass of tea, dropped it in the pocket of his nightshirt when he slept. Chewed it when he was bored.

Sworn Father Kojima was dead and Nanashi couldn't bring himself to wax sentimental. Too bad new boss, Uncle Yutaka, was an even bigger prick than the old boss.

* * *

While their fellow gangsters waited around the lobby of The Palace of the Sunfish, Koma took Nanashi and Amida to meet with Uncle Yutaka in the Gold Room. It was evidently a momentous occasion for Koma. He'd been surlier than normal. Sweat poured from him and a blister swelled on his lip; a sure sign of nerves. Everyone must be on their best behavior when Father arrived! Uncle Yutaka was number three in the Heron syndicate. Only the Chairman, their esteemed Father Akima, and his major domo were more powerful and they left everything up to Yutaka these days. Nanashi once heard Koma was afraid Uncle Yutaka didn't like him. From what Nanashi knew of Uncle Yutaka, he figured Koma's fear was reasonable.

Uncle Yutaka was old and fat. He wore amber-tinted shooting glasses and an ice water-blue suit from the 1960s. Heavily influenced by the James Bond movies of that era, he'd bankrolled a series of straight to video Tokyo and Hong Kong spy flicks, had established himself as a poor man's Albert Broccoli. His teeth were made of porcelain and his shaky hands were spackled with liver spots. He'd been to the hospital for three heart operations in the past five years. Haru claimed their uncle's heart was monitored by a pacemaker, but nobody knew for certain.

Uncle Yutaka enjoyed foreign cigarettes. He especially preferred Camels and Pall Malls, Benson & Hedges, and vintage brands like Lucky Strike. Everybody brought him cigarettes when they returned from travels abroad; it had become a minor contest between the brothers of the Heron to see whose exotic smokes Uncle would favor during his weekly audiences at the Palace of the Sunfish. Uncle smoked palm out and vented the exhaust from the sides of his mouth. Yutaka's tinted glasses pointed dead ahead and fooled most of the gang, but Nanashi caught Uncle watching him from the corners of his eyes. Uncle's eyes were yellow and pink and small like the eyes of a Komodo.

Nanashi hadn't been following the conversation, he never did; instead, he'd rolled up his sleeve and stuck his arm into the fish tank, patiently attempting to snag one of the snappers creeping in its depths. The weight of Uncle Yutaka's cold, reptilian appraisal made him nervous and fidgety. He churned the water and the fish scattered.

"No, no, Uncle. He's just a bit…distractible, is all." Koma stood at Uncle Yutaka's shoulder. His head was large and it sat directly on the wide collar of his canary-yellow suit. Uncle Yutaka was seated at his customary table with his cronies Ichiban and Akio, both of whom were old and withered, too shrunken for their antique suits and fedoras. They were sipping scotch and smoking lots of cigarettes. The air around them was blue and foul and made them seem to float. "He's an orphan. Uncle Kojima got him from -- Brother Amida, where did we find Nanashi?

"Kyoto," Amida said. "Drunk behind a garbage can." He casually guarded the entrance to the Gold Room. He was tall and lean and dressed in a sharp red blazer with cool black shades hanging from the breast pocket.

Koma said, "He used to drink a lot. A lot, a lot. He's much better now."

"Nanashi? What the shit kind of name is that?"

"It's just what everyone calls him," Koma said.

Nanashi's photo identification and birth certificate called him something else. However, those papers had been forged by yakuza agents in the government. Nanashi himself had purposefully buried his true name. His memories of childhood and youth prior to the blurred darkness of a years-long drunk were fragmentary and best forgotten.

Uncle Yutaka grunted. Smoke curled from his nostrils. "Kojima recruited him? Why on earth?" he said, as if it had never occurred to him before that moment.

"Who knows?" Koma said. "Uncle Kojima was inscrutable."

"Huh," Uncle Yutaka said. "Koma, I need to speak with you." That was the hint to clear out, so everyone except for Koma immediately filed from the room.

They stood around smoking and comparing cell phones until Koma rejoined them a few minutes later.

He said, "We've been ordered to pick up Muzaki. We'll do it tomorrow at the Fighting Dog."

"THE Muzaki? The wrestler?" Haru's eyes bulged.

"Don't get so excited. He's a has-been."

"Muzaki belongs to the Dragon. Why are we screwing with him?"

"Because Uncle says so, that's why."

"Yeah, but what for?"

"The guns we lost. The truck hijackings in the north. The plunger up that one brother's ass at the train station last year."

"The Dragons were behind all that? So, we take their mascot for revenge."

"Not revenge," Koma said. "Leverage. The Dragon repays us, or else. I think those assholes value him a great deal."

"Well, he's famous," Amida said, not that it needed saying. "And his nightclubs are excellent. Muzaki is a very respectable businessman. The Americans love him."

"*He's* American as far as I'm concerned," Haru said.

"Fuck them. I don't care. I'll pick you up in the morning."

"Does the Chairman know about this?" Nanashi had his suspicions on that score. The Yokohama bosses weren't supposed to do anything on this kind of scale the old men in Tokyo didn't approve first.

"It's between Heron and Dragon. Nobody in Tokyo needs to know nothing."

* * *

Koma swung by Nanashi's place the next morning in the long cobalt Cadillac his father shipped from Detroit as a coming of age present. Koma wore a lemon suit and a fancy wide-brimmed lemon hat that scraped the roof of the cab. Amida and Haru were in the backseat looking bored. As Koma drove, he mentioned a couple of brothers would meet them at the gym in a second car. Nanashi asked who Koma had called in. Koma said he hadn't called anybody, it was Uncle Nobukazu's order. Mizo and Jiki would be waiting at the gym in the second car was all Koma knew.

Mizo and Jiki? Nanashi shook his head in disgust. The Terrible Two were crazy. They were liable to do anything and answered to no one except Uncle Yutaka or Uncle Nobukazu, the latter of whom had rescued the men from an institution for the criminally deranged. Nanashi didn't trust Uncle Nobukazu's judgment. It was commonly known he'd acquired syphilis from some party girl and it was busily eating his brain.

Some speculated that Mizo and Jiki were twins, although Amida laconically pointed out that, "everybody with Down Syndrome looked alike" and no one could argue the point.

Nanashi lighted a cigarette and tried not to worry. He started to roll down the window, but the cab was already cloudy with blue smoke, so he didn't bother. He stared at the passing shop fronts as they declined and aged and gave way to impoverished warehouses and garages and self storage buildings.

Jiki and Mizo waited across the street from the gym in a parking lot. Both of them were fairly large and vaguely retarded. They eschewed the handsome suits of their more conservative yakuza brethren, or even the audacious pimp-suit stylings of new wave gangsters like Koma and his ilk, preferring pastel cargo pants and baggy, sleeveless tee shirts from Hong Kong outlet malls. Loose, formless clothing was just the thing for impromptu gang fights and scaling fences when fleeing the law. Nobody bothered to give them shit for violating the dress code.

Koma cruised alongside the duo, who were methodically thrashing a pair of high school kids. Everyone climbed out of the Cadillac and stood around to watch the action.

"Good morning, brothers," Mizo said as he cheerfully pressed his foot on the neck of a struggling youth. Jiki had thrown another boy facedown across the hood of the Honda. This kid wasn't moving, although he groaned occasionally. Jiki paused his search of the kid's pockets to wave at Koma. Nanashi guessed the kids were local dealers. Several foil packets and baggies were lined up on the hood, evidently confiscated by Jiki and Mizo.

"Yo," Mizo said to Nanashi and grinned. His mouth was crammed with silver braces. He worshipped at the altars of American hip-hop and gangster rap. "Hey, Nanashi, how's that sweet sister of yours, huh?"

Nanashi looked at him. He'd broken Mizo's foot when the hoodlum first joined the clan. Nanashi still drank at that point in his career and Mizo unwisely shot off his mouth. So Nanashi stomped his instep and then threw him over the balcony of the club they were partying at. It was a lazy attempt at a killing and Nanashi was much better when he so wished. Lucky for Mizo, the balcony was only a few feet above some hedges. He screeched and wailed all the way to the hospital. Everybody made fun of him for months until he got out of the cast and stopped limping.

"What the hell are you doing with these punks?" Koma said to Mizo. "Quit screwing the dog. We've got serious business."

"Very serious business," Jiki said. His laughter emerged as maniacal wheezing. As stupid as Jiki was, it could be difficult to tell if he was mocking Koma or agreeing with him. He slapped his victim on the buttocks and told him to get going. The kid was off like a shot.

Mizo sighed theatrically and took his foot off the neck of the other kid and let him run away. "Look at what those assholes tried to do! Look at this shit! They were trying to shortchange us. You don't mess with the yakuza. We *had* to beat them up." He swept the drug paraphernalia into his upended baseball cap and tossed the works into the Honda. "Okay. Ready to go."

"Is he here?" Nanashi said to Koma.

"Who? Muzaki?"

"Yeah."

"He's here. We got a guy inside. He called me on the way to your place. We're good, no need to worry."

The Fighting Dog was a house made of concrete blocks and sheet metal decorated by slashes of red and purple spray paint. The gym lay partially sunken beneath street level and despite its mean exterior and lousy accommodations, it remained one of the preeminent training facilities in the whole of Japan. Like the analogue four star hotels which hosted statesmen, movie stars, and emperors, in its forty years of history the Fighting Dog had served as training ground for scores of champion wrestlers, boxers, and martial artists. Nanashi thought it was definitely the kind of place where one might get one's ass kicked without much ceremony.

Muzaki was simply Muzaki, like Madonna and Sting. His legal name was Wesley Hallecker, born in Chicago in 1947. His father was an American businessman, his mother the youngest daughter of a doctor who'd maintained a practice in Kobe. Muzaki lived between the US and Japan until he graduated from Penn State. He eventually settled in Yokohama and became one of Japan's great wrestlers. Ever the crowd favorite for his phenomenal prowess and superhuman might, he'd also shrewdly concocted a personal mythology, a backstory that was the precursor to modern professional storylines in professional wrestling that included comic book personas with elaborately cartoonish biographies. Muzaki's own heroic tale claimed that he'd survived a shipwreck in the South Seas as a toddler and was subsequently raised by a lost tribe that ruled a chain of small, uncharted islands. This tribe allegedly practiced black magic and shrunk the heads of its enemies after drinking their blood and devouring their hearts. Muzaki was trained as a slayer of beasts and his exploits in the south were much celebrated until he was captured by men on a passing whaler and returned to civilization whereupon the government spent much time and effort rehabilitating him.

The fans loved it.

Father to numerous children, he'd married several times, most recently to a much younger American woman, an actress named Susan Stucky who hadn't acted in half a decade. An odd couple to be sure. The tabloids claimed they'd met when he rescued her from drowning at a casting party in Beverly Hills. She was floating face down near the bottom of a swimming pool and he'd dragged her out and revived her.

Everybody knew Muzaki the way everybody knew Ali or Pele. He was an institution and unlike a lot of other superstar athletes, he'd managed his money wisely and retired a wealthy man. He'd opened a chain of mixed martial arts gymnasiums, sporting goods stores, and invested in numerous nightclubs and warehouse properties. Muzaki's greatest and worst kept secret to financial success was his affiliation with the Dragon syndicate, number one rival of the Heron Clan. Muzaki, despite his waning celebrity, remained a sentimental investment of Miyami Tanaka, the Dragons' inestimable socho.

"Wait here," Nanashi said at the door, nodding at the crazy brothers. "Both of you."

"Huh?" Mizo thrust his chin forward. "Uncle Nobukazu said--"

"Wait here and watch the door."

"Why?" said Jiki.

"Because somebody has to do it."

"You watch the door, then."

"Shut up and watch the door," Koma said.

"What for?"

"Keep a lookout in case Tanaka's boys show up or something," Koma said. Of course, a bunch of Tanaka's boys could already be inside since the gym was a favorite hangout of Dragon foot soldiers, many of whom worshipped Muzaki like a god.

Jiki didn't say anything, just folded his arms in sullen resignation. Mizo rubbed his mouth. His cheeks became red. "Me and Jiki didn't come here to stand around while you guys --"

"Shut up," Koma said. He brushed past and went

inside.

Muzaki stood to greet Koma. They shook hands and exchanged pleasantries and Muzaki introduced the other men at the table -- a fight promoter, a lawyer, and a couple of trainers; nobody of importance. Nanashi hung back and watched them. He recognized Muzaki from the pictures and the old fight clips. The old man had gone to seed, but remained an impressive figure nonetheless. Squat as a fireplug, yet inordinately broad, his knuckles brushed his knees. There was a whole lot of muscle under all that flab. Koma, who'd grown rather stout himself, resembled a child by comparison.

Haru and Amida sidled next to Nanashi.

Haru said with the corner of his mouth, "You ever see his wife? The American? Oh boy. Oh man."

"The actress?" Amida said. "She's dead."

"No, she's alive. Susan something. Susan Stucky."

"Well, she doesn't act anymore. What was she in?"

"Lots of things."

"Yeah, but there was that one flick. Damn it, what was it called?"

"The gangster movie? The one where the Mafia blew her up on the yacht? There's a tragedy. What a waste. That two piece white bikini she ran around in almost gave me a heart attack."

"She was an ice bitch."

"Oh yeah. Oh boy."

"That big ugly bastard is hitting that? I am in the wrong business."

Muzaki swiveled his lumpy head their direction as if he'd caught their whispers.

"Man, he's big," Amida said. "My father swore he

was in Osaka the night Muzaki broke Ostreshinger's back. I wonder if I can get his autograph."

"Sure you can," Haru said. "Didn't he kill the German? I thought he did. It was in the papers."

"No, no. Muzaki just hurt him. Ostreshinger was in a wheelchair for a few years. He died in a home. Respiratory failure."

"Exactly. Which was courtesy of Muzaki fucking him up, right? So, Muzaki killed him."

"If you look at it that way, yeah. Muzaki killed the shit out of that German. Kind of sad. If he hadn't killed the guy, he probably wouldn't have retired so soon after."

"You think Muzaki retired because he felt guilty over what happened?" Haru shook his head. "No way. Who cares what happens to one of those bastards? It was business. Muzaki got out because he was becoming a slob. Look at him over there."

"I'm looking, believe me. How are we gonna get him in the car?"

"It's not like we're gonna stuff him in the trunk."

"We're not? Oh, good."

"Anyway, we got an axe."

In the end Muzaki smiled hugely and came along, docile as could be. Nanashi, whose job description included fretting over such details, didn't like it at all.

* * *

Koma drove inland. The day was bright and warm. Nanashi sat on the front passenger side, angled so he could see the rearview mirror. Haru and Muzaki sat in back. Mizo, Jiki, and Amida paced them in the second car.

"Is it far?" Muzaki said as the city eventually dropped from sight behind them and they crossed mile after mile of rice and bean fields. "If it's far, you should know I've got a kidney problem." He shifted his bulk uncomfortably.

"It's far," Koma said. He drove fast, pedal to the floorboard when traffic allowed. Koma was a formula car nut. He seemed to think he'd watched enough grand prix's to drive like Hakkinen or Schumacher.

"Ah. About my kidneys --"

"You can go in this," Koma said, swishing the remnants of a liter bottle of cola.

"Don't worry, Muzaki-san," Haru said. "We'll stop along the way. Koma has his own kidney problems and there's only one bottle, right?"

"I should've made you ride with the mongoloid twins," Koma said. "Let's have some music." He turned on the radio and began fiddling with the dial.

A black cloud swooped in directly overhead and blocked out the sun. Rain pinged from the windows and obliterated the highway markings.

"Haru says you are a fighter," Muzaki said.

"Eh? Me?" Nanashi startled, realizing the big man was speaking to him. "Not really. I'm too old."

"Too old?"

"I'm thirty-three."

"That isn't so bad. Not if you're tough."

"When I was a boy I trained in a dojo, that's all."

They regarded each other in the mirror. Muzaki's features were brutish and scarred. His skull was shaped like an anvil. His ears had contracted to small, fleshy knobs. His nose was a deflated bump of impacted cartilage. He reached forward and grasped Nanashi's shoulder and squeezed. The power in his hand was enough to make Nanashi queasy.

Muzaki said, "But you still train. You're built like a good, sturdy light-heavyweight. You've never been in the ring?"

"No. I trained for…habit, I guess." Nanashi lit another cigarette to cover his unease. He'd seen enough clips of Muzaki strangling his hapless foes. Muzaki was famous for hip throws and sleeper holds. "The Savage" had been one of his many ring names. He'd dressed in bear skins, on occasion. Real skins.

"Habit?" Muzaki settled and the entire rear seat creaked beneath his weight. "May I have a cigarette?"

"Say, Muzaki-san, have one of my mine." Haru reached inside his coat.

"No, thank you. Nanashi?"

Nanashi turned awkwardly in his seat and handed Muzaki a cigarette. Haru quickly lighted it for Muzaki.

"Thank you." Muzaki coughed a bit. "Ack. It's been years since I smoked one of these.

"Why start up again?" Nanashi said.

"Isn't it tradition for the condemned to get a last cigarette?"

"Don't be so melancholy," Koma said. "We're just going for a ride. Jesus."

"Yes. Where is this place, again?"

"Inland," Koma gestured vaguely.

"Inland…" Muzaki nodded to himself.

"In the mountains. We'll stay at the lodge tonight."

"Oh?"

"You'll enjoy it," Haru said. "It's nice. I take Koma's girlfriend there all the time."

"Hey! Watch your mouth!" Koma said over his

shoulder and almost swerved into the ditch. Haru chuckled and slipped a set of headphones over his ears.

A chill crept into the car despite their mingled breath and cigarette smoke. Cold air rushed through the vent and over Nanashi's knees. They glided among hills. Every piece of landscape lay abstracted by water rushing over the windshield. Koma engaged the headlights and it was as if they were driving into an endless tunnel. Nanashi remembered killing ants as a boy with his brother's Swiss Army knife -- first with the magnifying glass, then the blade. He'd poured water into their nests, watched black torrents of workers and soldiers tumbling in the rivulets. He envisioned God's thumb poised over the Cadillac.

Late in the afternoon, they left the highway and followed a single lane along a fast-moving stream that had carved a gorge of black stones and flint-ribbed cliffs over the aeons. Rushes swirled along the cut-banks where the churn and froth subsided to misty vapor. Bamboo trees swayed, and the shadows of bamboo trees swayed also, and when Koma stopped the car so Haru could snap a few photographs of the waterfalls, Nanashi went to the edge of the road and stared down into the gulf of trees and bushes and rocks. The rain had slackened to a drizzle. His hair hung lank across his eyes; his tie drooped, a sodden cord.

Birds called angrily from the forest depths. Or ghosts made angry bird cries from the forest depths, urging trespassers to turn away, to make for the well-traveled roads, the safety of highway markings, telephone poles and lights, the comfort of multitudes. Nanashi had come here once before in the tenure of

Uncle Kojima, had stood in this very spot on the crumbling precipice while his brethren took photos and smoked cigarettes and passed around hip flasks of brandy, and he'd listened to the strange arboreal chorus. He thought this time there were more voices out there among the trees. He tapped his prosthesis against his silver eyetooth.

The lodge itself crowded the summit of a butte overlooking the upper falls of the gorge. Matasui Hot Springs was an amalgam of old eastern pagoda and Nineteenth Century French chalet; very rustic and very exclusive. The parking lot notched the hillside; a rusty guardrail demarcated a sheer drop of at least sixty meters. Theirs were the only vehicles in the lot.

Mossy flagstone steps made a series of switchbacks up to the main building. The seven went single file, Nanashi at the rear. He gripped the slick wooden rail and scanned the road until it dwindled far below into the misty woods. He didn't think they'd been followed, but it paid to be cautious. Powerful forces surrounded Muzaki, after all.

* * *

Nanashi disliked the proprietors, an obsequious, elderly couple from Tokyo. The couple presided at the front door with a contingent of young men who fought amongst themselves over a handful of valises and overnight bags the Herons had brought along. Nanashi overheard Haru explain to Muzaki that the Herons owned a significant stake in the lodge. The details were cloudy; Nanashi knew the establishment made a nice honest front for the syndicate, and a terrific place for the bosses to relax and conduct business far from prying eyes in the city. Indeed, the city literally crawled with spies; they scuttled in every nook and cranny, *like cockroaches*, as Uncle Kojima had said a dozen times a day. He'd been right, too. Old, stately Kojima, collector of walking canes, fingers, and women -- shot ninety-six times by a pair of goons wielding Chinese submachine guns, right there in his own satin sheets on his own enormous bed. What an ignominious end for a modern day warlord.

The twins were given custody of Muzaki. They flanked him like attack dogs while he inspected the rather expansive foyer as it opened into a common room decorated with plush furniture, bamboo pots, and a stone fireplace already crackling behind ornamental grates. Here and there were marble lamps and apparently authentic statuary (arms and heads were broken off!), and on a carpeted dais, a baby grand piano gleamed like a piece of black ivory. A long, shiny bar formed an L near sliding doors that led onto a patio, which extended beyond the cliff and into open space. Of course, Koma, Amida, and Haru made directly for the bar where a tall, bald man in a silk shirt and suspenders was already lining the counter with shots of whiskey.

Nanashi stepped out to make a brief tour of the grounds. He followed the crushed stone path around the perimeter of the lodge and several outbuildings. These latter were private bungalows, and all appeared empty, their doors locked and windows shuttered. He peered through the glass, and was greeted by darkness and silence. Behind the central building was a storage shed and a low timber building that snugged into the hill. A sign on the door marked it as the bath house. More paths spiraled from the central axis into the shrubbery. It was rapidly becoming too dim to appraise the situation much further, so he went inside. He selected a table adjacent the terrace and told the unctuous proprietor, who'd slithered over with a bottle and glasses, to away with the booze and fetch him green tea and honey. His companions were enjoying themselves immensely -- they clustered around Muzaki, who seemed to be involved in teaching them a card trick, or passing around a wallet photograph.

A few minutes later, Jiki and Mizo came over, their captive in tow. "Hey, you watch this guy for a while," Jiki said, pointing to Muzaki.

"Yeah," Mizo said. "We're going to get wasted."

Muzaki settled his hulk across from Nanashi. He smiled, cave-like.

The proprietor returned with tea and poured it for Nanashi and Muzaki and hung around rubbing his hands together entirely too long until Nanashi drew his revolver from its shoulder holster and set it on the table. The proprietor went away.

"So." Muzaki sipped his tea. "We wait."

Nanashi nodded. He holstered the gun and smoothed his wet hair against his skull.

Darkness slipped over the land. The rain was back and it had brought the wind. He shivered despite the warmth of the lodge. The guffaws and raucous cries of his comrades at the bar reminded him of the jeering birds, and he felt strangely alone.

"I like you, Nanashi," Muzaki said.

"Thank you. I admire you, as well." In the awkward silence that followed, Nanashi poured the remainder of the tea. He snapped his fingers at the proprietor, who carefully lurked just beyond eavesdropping vantage. The man scurried to fetch another pot.

"You've seen my fights?"

"Oh, certainly. My father never missed one. We watched them together." Nanashi didn't think about his previous life when he could avoid it. This memory knifed through the fog, the denials, and incised itself upon his mind.

"Ah. I am glad to hear such things in my declining years," Muzaki said.

"In fact, my father was something of a scholar regarding the lives of the great wrestlers. He intended to write a book one day. He studied your biography closely. And the documentary that was done in the 1980s."

"Such a bit of nonsense and fluff. I was vainglorious in my youth."

"With reason." Nanashi was impressed with the big man's recovery from the anxious journey. He appeared altogether more relaxed and collected than his circumstances warranted. The Herons possessed a reputation for casual malice and sadism. Every gang in the land knew of the ghouls Mizo and Jiki, the Terrible Two. Surely Muzaki knew, as well. "How do you come by fearlessness?"

"Is such a thing possible?"

"Well, then. How do you come by the illusion of fearlessness? That is arguably a more formidable accomplishment."

"Fear arises from the unknown. I now understand my situation perfectly. Besides, I am not truly here in the larger sense. None of us are. I am curious, though. Why is it that most gangsters talk with their mouths closed? All that grunting makes it difficult to understand what they are saying."

"Makes them sound tough. Like bad guys in the movies." Nanashi glanced at his associates--gibbons, snarling and strutting. Saddened, he flicked his gaze toward the darkness beyond the terrace. "It has occurred to me, more and more, that this existence is one of reckless waste. We labor in futility."

"Ha! My friend...such a morose comment. And you're completely sober."

"I think we were all better off when I was a happy drunk."

"The world adores happy drunks and it deifies fools. Did I not play the buffoon in the ring? No one really loved me until the costumes, the play acting and charades that replaced the real blood and tears of my sacred profession. When I abandoned sport and became a caricature, I ascended unto that most sublime tier of entertainers. I once dressed as a bat, like a *luchador*. Oh, the agony."

Nanashi remembered the bat costume, indeed. And the fake metal chairs used as bludgeons, the fake blows, red dye and caramelized sugar. His father had stopped watching by then, had stuffed his notes and papers into a box and pretended he'd never been particularly interested in the first place.

"It is strange that you ended up with these thugs," Muzaki said. "Something wondrous and terrible occurred in your youth."

"I was discovered living a vagrant's life in an alley. Heron family rescued me, redeemed me."

"Like baby Moses discovered in his basket. What came before the basket?"

"I'm the Man with No Name. I drink, brood, kill. The past is immaterial."

"Ah. Fuck the past!"

"Fuck the past!"

There was a scuffle at the bar. Mizo, red-faced and swearing, clutched Haru's tie. Haru waved a flip knife. There was laughter as the others pulled them apart and shoved glasses into their hands in an attempt to drown their whiskey-fueled aggression by the counterintuitive method of killing fire with fire. Nanashi said, "The future is unwritten. I could stand and walk through the door and disappear in any direction. Why is that so difficult to remember in the present?"

"Because death and destruction follow the Man with No Name wherever he goes. This is the natural order of the universe." Muzaki's smile was strange. His scars seemed to become more livid and to stretch in discomfiting ways. For a moment, the essential atavism of his countenance was accentuated; its intelligence and *humanity,* receding into the pits of his eyes.

Nanashi concentrated on the darkness. "Koma keeps me around because I am steady. I never lose my head when trouble comes."

"A helpful talent in your business."

"Yes." Nanashi shifted his gaze and all was again well with Muzaki's face. "There are six bullets. I could fire them in the order of the danger my brethren present. Two for Amida. Two for Haru. If I were lucky, I might strike Jiki in the heart or neck and need but a single shot. That would leave Koma and Mizo. Could you cross the floor and take one of them before he gathered his wits? I would suggest Koma as he has fewer to gather."

Muzaki signaled. "Mr. Innkeeper, bring my friend

and I a drink. Something strong. Something to fuck the past before it fucks him."

Nanashi's drink came -- a cup of jet, pungent alcohol. "This is my seventh year sober." He balanced the cup in his palm, then gulped the whiskey all at once. Sweet ever loving hell, it was good. He trembled. The innkeeper promptly poured again. "Uh, oh," Nanashi said and made the booze disappear.

"To the hells with sobriety." Muzaki upended his cup into a mouth missing several teeth. "We cannot afford the luxury of a clear mind." He removed a piece of paper from his pocket. He leaned across the table. His breath was foul. "Take this. It's different from the bad one I showed your brothers. Keep it under your pillow when you sleep tonight."

Nanashi examined the paper. It had been crumpled and smoothed a hundred times. It was yellow and spackled with oil spots, or water stains. "What is this?"

"The beautiful thing that awaits us all. Focus on the imperfections in the paper and slowly count to five. Then close your eyes, but gently, don't squeeze them shut, and turn your face toward the lamp over there."

"I wonder what the point of this is."

"Haven't you ever faced the sun and traced the veins inside your eyelids?"

"Not recently."

"You'll understand. Start counting."

"Perhaps now is not the time for riddles, Muzaki-san."

"Yes, it is. Here's one -- I once had seven brothers. Like Saturn, father ate my brothers, but my mother was clever. She swaddled a suckling pig and fed it to him in my place."

"That seems more like a mystery than a riddle...or a joke of poor taste."

"Ha! And as Polyphemus was taken with Odysseus, your mirth delights me."

"You should decide between the Romans and the Greeks. Will you devour me last?"

"Are you drunk already, brave Ronin? Come, indulge me. Look at the paper and count." He gave Nanashi a friendly slap to help him concentrate.

Nanashi concentrated on the blotches on the paper -- some were dark and sufficiently ominous to have escaped from some doctor's inkblot book. He counted to five, then closed his eyes and tilted his face toward the lamp hanging near their table. Its light chased shadows across his eyelids. "Shit!" He caught the edge of the table to keep from toppling.

"Most people see Jesus."

"Where did you get this? What is it?"

"An American gave me one of those when I was a boy. He was one of my father's associates -- a military person, I suspect. So many of father's friends were, after all. We'd retired outside after dinner on a pleasant summer evening. The man asked me if I liked magic. He showed me a piece of paper much like this one, and told me what to do. My father wasn't pleased. They had an argument and the man apologized. He winked at me behind Father's back and let me keep the paper to play with, to show the other boys at school."

"I didn't see Jesus." Nanashi's vision still swam red. "Or the Buddha."

"No? Not everyone does. What was it, then?"

"The other one."

"You are the kindest of them. You are also the worst of them. It would be easy to love or hate you,

Nanashi-san. That is why I am going to give you a rabbit's prayer. My gift to a fellow traveler."

"A rabbit's prayer."

Muzaki nodded gravely. "Remember not to fuck up when the moment arrives. You'll have one chance."

"Huh?" Nanashi said. The booze was hitting him like a truck.

"Hey, Nanashi!" Amida called from the bar. His collar was open, his usually immaculate hair was disheveled. "Come join us in the springs. Hurry up!"

"Oh, do let's," Muzaki said as Amida staggered away through an open panel on the opposite end of the room.

Through this side doorway and down some steps, they exited the lodge and made their way along a path to the timber bathhouse. Inside was a low-ceilinged cave Nanashi was sure he'd dreamt of before. Steam rose from an oblong pool. The bottom and sides of the pool were composed of smoothed, natural stone. Green and blue light rippled against the walls and the men's shadows capered there, like silhouettes cast by a magic lantern.

"In feudal times this was a sacred cave," Muzaki said, and his voice resonated eerily and Nanashi had a flash of Kirk Douglas confronting the Cyclops in its lair. "It is rumored that powerful samurai travelled here to bathe in preparation for important battles and duels of honor."

Nanashi found the enclosure oppressive. The steam, the closeness of the walls, combined to evoke a profound disquiet. He watched his clan brothers splashing and wrestling, all of them inked in elaborate tattoos from the neck down -- their flesh crawled with snakes and herons and scorpions and mythical beasts, all in hues of red and green and black. Except for Jiki; he leaped in fully clothed, and his shirt billowed around his chest.

"My manager threw a party for me here in 1987. This was before your clan took over the place. There were girls back then."

The house servants had been shooed away by Koma, so Nanashi undressed himself. He unbuttoned his shirt. He folded his clothes and placed them on a bench. He wrapped his revolver in a towel and set it atop the clothes. The water was the temperature of blood and it lapped at his throat. His own needlework was intricate and expensive, commissioned to one of the greatest tattoo artists in all of Japan. The others, especially Koma, were jealous despite the fact he'd earned the illustrations by dint of committing more violence than all but the most aged soldiers of the Heron.

Nanashi never truly enjoyed his profession nor its magnificent rewards. He was simply ruthless; during conflict, remoteness stole over him, as if a hole had opened in his heart. Blood flowed, ink flowed. Violence and Irezumi, vines on a rail. Seven years of mayhem had afforded him a second skin more glorious than the infant first. He fantasized about the effort it might require to remove those layers, needle prick by needle prick. He wondered how much of himself remained underneath.

Everyone stopped when Muzaki, frightful in his nakedness, waded into the pool until he mostly submerged, a massive bullfrog, exposing only his eyes and sloping forehead. He farted and bubbles wobbled to the surface. Jiki screeched laughter, and moments later the clan surrounded Muzaki. Muzaki reared, spitting streams of water at them, gently pushing them beneath the surface when they ventured within the span of his meaty arms.

Nanashi's nausea intensified. He turned his back to them and pressed his forehead against the slick rim of the pool. He saw the American actor driving the sharpened pole into the giant's eye, again and again.

* * *

Koma assigned Nanashi, Amida, and Muzaki to a sleeping chamber. Amida volunteered for first watch, having shaken off much of his previous drunkenness. He produced a deck of cards and offered their captive a game of *Uta-garuta*.

Nanashi lay upon a mat in the corner, listening to the whispered recitations of each *waka* until their voices diminished to white noise. He dreamed of kneeling on rice paper in the ornate home of dearly deceased Uncle Kojima. He was shirtless and the room was cold, but sweat already slickened the hilt of the Tanto knife in his fist. Light flickered from candles, obscuring the faces of his brethren, who gathered around him in funereal silence. Uncle Kojima sat in a padded chair several paces in front of Nanashi. Uncle's chair had been situated directly beneath a hanging lamp. The old man was dressed in a conservative black suit. He rested an elbow on the arm of the chair, hand covering his mouth. Probably to hide his smile. Uncle Kojima enjoyed pain and suffering. To his left was a small wooden table; on the table, a jar. Uncle Kojima caressed the jar; he slowly drummed his fingers on the metal lid.

Nanashi looked down at the knife. He tried not to

consider the jar as he folded his left hand into a partial fist, leaving the pinky exposed. He pressed the edge of the blade against the second joint and drew a long breath --

-- he was flying over forested mountains, skimming treetops. Wind whipped his face and the light was flat and grimy. He landed in a clearing on a steep hillside. Moss-covered boulders strew the hill and continued into the brush. He took a step and something crunched under his heel -- a human skull. There were skulls everywhere; a vast, moldering carpet of them, and ribcages and leg bones mostly subsumed by the damp earth. Amid the bones lay rotted articles of clothing, backpacks, remnants of camp tents, tires from vehicles so old the rubber had melted. Dread overcame him, rooted him in his tracks, and he groaned. He knew if archeologists dug into this hillside they'd unearth a fossil record of carnage that burrowed into the yawning mouth of antiquity. Someone whistled from the trees; a soft, lilting tune that was answered from several hidden locations. The whistling grew louder, accompanied by cracking branches. Men wearing antlers, their bulky torsos covered in animal skins, shambled forth. They hooted and whistled a song he almost recognized; something incongruously popular, something urban, which made it all the more awful. One of the misshapen brutes waved--

-- Nanashi plunged from a terrible height into water. At first he drifted in lightless depths, arms and legs spread loosely, and his previous panic melted, replaced by a sense of finality, of release. Gradually, his surroundings brightened, exposed by an unearthly, muted radiance that came from many directions at once. He followed the bubbles of his own escaping breath upward and saw an inverted bed of fleshy kelp, or soft, white tubers, swaying as the water in the jar sloshed. The white tubers had faces he began to recognize when a monstrously large hand, distorted by the curved glass walls, closed around the jar and all was dark --

-- and Nanashi fell back into the sleeping chamber, frozen upon his mat. Someone in another room played a stringed instrument, plucking at the chords and humming the tune he'd heard whistled by the mountain phantoms.

A single ray of lamplight filtered down to illuminate the prisoner Muzaki in profile, seated cross-legged near the door, head bowed to his breast. He wore a thick towel wrapped around his midsection and he twitched with each discordant note struck by the neighboring musician. Nanashi realized that despite the pain of his seized muscles, the hyper-clarity of his senses, this was another part of the dream. The music was a figment -- it faded in and out, yet Muzaki twitched in metronome and a cotton cloud muffled and nullified the chorus of snores, groans, and flatulence of the sleeping gangsters as they lay scattered like dolls beyond paper thin walls and sliding panels.

Sound contracted around Nanashi, reduced to his thumping heart, his labored panting. A fly alighted on Nanashi's cheek, drawn by his sweat, and just then nearby Muzaki's arms flew wide and his head thrust back so the sinews of his neck were taut. A seam opened him, bisected his flesh from temple to toe. The man divided, skin and bone elongating until twin halves became separate wholes, yoked at the spine by a length of ganglia. Then each whole divided again and soon there was a daisy chain of howling Muzaki's elongating toward infinity.

Nanashi was paralyzed, yet fully aware, as blood poured across the floor and rushed toward his gaping mouth - -

* * *

The morning was overcast. Nanashi sat on the chilly terrace and ate a bowl of white rice and drank several cups of black coffee laced with brandy. Normally, tea was his preference. However, today was a coffee and liquor sort of day. The proprietor owned an espresso machine. He made the coffee into syrup, Turkish style, per Nanashi's specifications.

The rest of the gang were inside. Through the glass, he saw Koma slouched at a corner table, cradling his head and talking on the house phone. He was conferring with his bookie about the horse races -- he scribbled on slips of paper, hunting through his pockets every few seconds for more of them. Gambling was his particular area of expertise, although he'd never been wise enough to avoid becoming addicted to the very vice he peddled. He owed money everywhere and people had begun to whisper. Apparently the latest news wasn't good -- he barked at anyone who came close. His voice barely reached Nanashi, as if he and the others were calling out from a distant valley.

Amida and Haru stepped onto the terrace to smoke cigarettes. "Good morning," Haru said. He lighted two cigarettes and walked over and handed one to Nanashi. "My head is swollen from too many drinks. I hardly remember anything from last night. Good thing you gave up drinking, huh? You could be suffering like me."

Nanashi smiled. He wondered if Koma or the maniac twins had noticed him downing liquor. Koma would be quite alarmed if he learned that his subordinate had fallen off the wagon. Koma might decide to cut his losses if Nanashi became so reckless as he'd been when they first rehabilitated him in the bad old days. Koma was looking for the slightest excuse. Nanashi didn't really give a damn one way or the other. That bothered him a little.

Haru's face was doughy with exhaustion. He rubbed his eye. "I feel like shit, Nanashi. I didn't sleep a wink. What about you?"

"I slept like a baby."

"Yeah?"

"Uh-huh."

"Damn. I want to grow up and be just like you. You're a cool customer. Nothing bothers you. Hey, Amida. How'd you sleep last night?"

"Like shit," Amida said. He looked as bad as Haru.

"Me too! But our friend here, he slept the night through. Fresh as a daisy!"

"He doesn't drink. If I didn't drink, I'd be fresh as a daisy too."

"Maybe I should give up liquor. What are you drinking?" Haru gestured at Nanashi's cup.

"Coffee."

"Yeah? Maybe that's what I should do -- drink coffee, like you."

"Maybe you should."

"What?"

Koma yelled from inside, "Get Nanashi in here!"

"Koma's asking for you," Haru said. "Could I try that?" He took Nanashi's coffee and sipped. He made a face. "How can you drink this stuff?"

"Where's Muzaki?"

"Jiki and Mizo took him for a walk. Muzaki walks two miles every morning. Wouldn't know it from his looks."

Nanashi took Muzaki's yellow paper from his pocket, careful not to unfold it this time. He stared at it a moment before lighting a corner with the tip of his cigarette. He held the paper at arm's length and watched it burn to a crisp, its ashes scattered by the breeze.

Haru said, "Did Muzaki show you the trick?"

"Which one?"

"The one where you stare at some spots and then close your eyes. I saw Buddha!"

Koma shouted an epithet.

"Koma wants you," Amida said. He leaned against the rail so that his hair hung over the gulf. His voice was weak. "Please don't piss him off this early in the morning. My head feels like a kettle drum."

"Your *ass* looks like two bongos! You need to exercise." Haru slapped his own buttock for emphasis. "My girlfriend makes me work out with her to *Bunz of Iron*. She owns the whole series. It's a miracle."

"You watch workout videos with your girlfriend?"

"Why not? My ass looks great, doesn't it?"

"Yeah, it does."

Nanashi stubbed his cigarette in the saucer and walked inside. He sat across from Koma who was clutching a fistful of the betting slips. More lay on the table, while others had fallen to the floor.

Koma's bloodshot eyes bulged dangerously and the blister on his lip was ripe as a grape. His dirty breakfast dishes hadn't been cleared away and the ashtray was already half full. He slammed the phone and wiped his sweaty face with a handkerchief. "When Jiki and Mizo get back, we're all going for a drive to the quarry." He said this without glancing up, as if his gruffness disguised shame.

"When did Uncle Yutaka call?"

"I don't know. An hour ago."

Nanashi stared at the top of Koma's skull where the hair was relentlessly thinning. "Are we sure about this?"

"Yeah, yeah. Uncle was clear. We take him to the quarry."

"Okay."

"Okay with you? Our orders meet with your approval?" Koma stuffed the slips into his coat pocket. "Go on. Get the fuck away from me. You're giving me a headache. Hold on. Get those for me." He pointed at the slips scattered around his feet and glowered while Nanashi crouched, leaning under the table, and scooped them into his hand. "Okay, okay. Give them here. *Now* beat it."

Nanashi checked his watch. He snapped his fingers at one of the young waiters loitering about and ordered him to shine his shoes. Normally, he shined his own shoes, ironed his own clothes. The kid's indolence, his casual jocularity, irritated him. He phoned Yuki and apologized immediately for waking her. She mumbled with exhaustion, wondered if he'd be home soon. Her boss was being an asshole. He laughed and told her it was going around, and promised to pick her up at the end of her next shift. Her answers were vague and far apart, so he said goodbye, made kissing noises, and broke the connection. The kid shining his shoes smirked before averting his gaze. Nanashi toyed with the idea of kicking him in the throat, making him an example for the other little punks. That's what Amida or Haru would've done. Instead, he didn't tip.

* * *

They got on the road again -- same arrangement as the previous day. This time, no one talked. Nanashi sensed the change in his associates -- they were strung tight now that word of Uncle Yutaka's decision had passed among them. Koma drove with both hands, white-knuckling the wheel. Haru put on his headphones and stared out the window. Muzaki seemed oblivious to the tension. He yawned and leaned back, hands folded behind his neck, eyes half closed.

Nanashi lighted a cigarette, grateful no one was interested in conversation. He sneaked glances at Muzaki in the rearview mirror, wondering how much of the heavy-lidded slothfulness was an act. Certainly, he was no one's fool. Could he really be at peace? What did such a thing feel like? Already, Nanashi's throat was dry. The need for a drink was an itch in the back of his mind. He hadn't fallen from the wagon -- he'd leaped.

Their route was circuitous and took them through a series of off-ramps and access roads to a plain of broken slabs of granite. Decrepit paved lots looped as fractured geometric patterns into the distance. Koma parked among weeds and crushed glass and flattened bottle caps at the rim of a manmade crater. An abandoned derrick rusted down there amid pools of orange alkaline and pieces of ruined machinery, and rocks and gravel.

Amida rolled alongside. The doors clanked open and everyone got out, stretched, and lighted cigarettes with fancy lighters. Haru started snapping pictures, gesturing for his comrades to strike poses. They stood around making nervous small talk until Koma gave Amida a look. Amida dropped his cigarette and ground it under the heel of his loafer. He stuck his hands into his pockets and shuffled over to where Muzaki was peering into the pit. He stood so close to Muzaki, their shoulders brushed. A slender blade dropped from Amida's sleeve and glittered in his hand.

Nanashi sat on the bumper of the Cadillac and folded his arms. His mind began to empty. The light was reddening. Had they driven so long? A seagull drifted past. Yuki, sweet Yuki, would be dressing for work. She'd be putting on her cocktail dress, dusting her cheeks with the barest hint of glitter. Nanashi's father patted the couch -- on television the great Muzaki raised an opponent overhead, and the black and white crowd cheered. *He* wasn't the one about to meet his fate, so why was it *his* life flashing before his eyes?

Muzaki laughed at something Amida said. He glanced over his shoulder at Nanashi and winked. He casually grabbed Amida by the belt, lifted him to his shoe tips, and flung him into space. Nanashi was so shocked at the slapstick aspect of the event, he chuckled. The other men froze in a tableau of department store manikins, cigarettes poised near their slack mouths, and Haru's camera fixed to his eye. Muzaki ignored everyone, leaning farther out, hands on knees, to regard hapless Amida's earthward trajectory.

The camera clicked. Jiki squawked and hopped into action, brandishing a steel jack handle with tape wrapped around the grip. He smashed Muzaki in the base of his skull with a hollow, ringing *thunk*. Muzaki didn't flinch, so Jiki tried again, starting from his ankles and looping the jack handle in an overhand strike, as if he were splitting a log. This time, Muzaki took a small step and pitched forward and dropped from view. That broke the group paralysis, and in a stream, Jiki, Mizo, and Haru went whooping and scrambling after him.

Koma ran to the edge, fancy lemon hat in hand. He pulled at his hair with his other hand and made frequent unhappy exclamations about the scene below. A series of *pops* echoed from the pit. Then three more, much lighter ones followed by a bunch of shouting. Nanashi recognized the first gunshots as belonging to Haru's .32 automatic. Haru had originally bought it for his girlfriend as a birthday present. She didn't like guns and he lost his own pistol into a canal while drunk, so now he carried the puny .32 and hoped no one would notice to give him shit -- which everyone had, naturally. The second volley came from a .22 pistol, although it was a mystery who might be strapped with such an embarrassingly trivial caliber weapon. The .32 fired again. The shouting resumed, accompanied by cries of pain, but no more gunshots.

"What the fuck! What the fuck! Doesn't anybody in this gang carry a *real* gun?" Koma sounded as if he were going out of his mind. He grabbed a chunk of loose rock and hurled it. "You fucking idiots! You can't shoot a rhino with a pellet gun!" He ran back to Nanashi. His face was shiny with rage and terror. "You've got a cannon -- get your ass down there and do something! Blow his fucking head off!"

"No," Nanashi said. He stared at his shoes. The very notion of departing the comforting gravity of the car bumper made him sick and dizzy.

You'll have a rabbit's chance.

"What? Go! Go!" When Nanashi didn't answer, Koma screeched and began slapping him about the head and shoulders with his hat. "What's wrong with you? Have you lost your nerve? Are you some kind of chicken?"

Nanashi shielded his face from the blows. He wept in pain and humiliation. Koma kept slapping him with the ridiculous hat. He only stopped when Mizo jogged past them to the rear of the other car and sprang the trunk. The bow-legged little man grabbed a red fireman's axe. He huffed and puffed. His baggy clothes were splattered with blood. His face was swollen and agonized like a man in the throes of an orgasm.

Koma said, "What the fuck is going on down there? Whose axe is that?" Mizo shook his head, too winded to speak. He scurried off. Koma put his hat on and walked heavily to the edge of the quarry. He stood there for a while, observing the ruckus. His shoulders slumped. Eventually it became quiet, and he said, "Holy fuck," a few times. He walked back to the car and stood before Nanashi. His eyes were glassy. "Holy fuck," he said. "Good thing somebody brought an axe, I guess." He joined Nanashi on the bumper. He dug around in his jacket and removed a pack of cigarettes, and cursed to find it empty. As he balled the pack in his fist, his cell phone began to play a tinny melody.

Nanashi stood and moved away from the Cadillac to compose himself. He wiped his eyes on his sleeve and blew his nose. Behind him, Koma finally answered the phone. After a long pause, he said in a perfectly calm voice, *"What do you mean it's off?"*

Part Two

The Maze of Knives

They journeyed into darkness.

Nanashi drove because Koma was far too shaken by contemplating his possible fate once they returned to the city. Haru tended Amida in the back seat. Amida's suit was tattered. He'd broken his arm in the fall. His nose was crushed into a jellified lump. He'd bled so severely blood coagulated in a bib on his chest, caked his face like a rubber mask. He moaned whenever Nanashi changed lanes too quickly, or hit a bump, or touched the radio volume. Koma moaned too.

Jiki and Mizo were stuck in the Honda with Muzaki's mutilated corpse. Mizo was driving. His headlights trailed a few car-lengths back and Nanashi distracted himself from fantasies of impending doom by speculating about the current conversation going on in the Honda. They, being idiots, meant this line of conjecture didn't go far. The last he'd seen them, the two were laughing hysterically, gore soaking their clothes. Jiki had made a comment that provoked Mizo into chasing him around with the axe until Koma screamed that he was going to have their fingers cut off if they didn't shut the fuck up.

Instead, Nanashi's mind went to Muzaki's bulk wrapped in a tarp and rammed into the back of the car. It had taken forty-five minutes and Mizo, Jiki, and Haru's combined efforts to drag him from the pit. Nanashi was powerless to tear his gaze away from the whole clumsy, awful mess, right up until Haru kept slamming the door on Muzaki's shoeless foot as it dangled. Uncle Yutaka wanted the corpse returned to headquarters, although he didn't say why. Nanashi suspected it was because he and Uncles Nobukazu and Ichiban were sentimental enough to think the famous wrestler deserved a proper ceremony. This displeased Haru, Jiki, and Mizo, who unanimously agreed that burying Muzaki in the quarry and pretending none of it had ever happened was the best plan. Amida probably agreed with the consensus view, but his grunts and gurgles were unintelligible.

The way Nanashi figured, all of them were already dead men. Dead rabbits, if one preferred.

"What a day," Koma said. He turned on the radio and scanned through the channels. He turned the radio off. He suddenly beamed like a child. "You are in a lot of trouble when we get home. Uncle is going to be angry with you. This is all your fault, Nanashi-san. He will blame you completely." This seemed to give him comfort and he patted Nanashi's arm affectionately. "Got a cigarette?"

Nanashi pushed in the dash lighter. When it popped, he stuck two cigarettes into his mouth and lighted them. He handed one to Koma. The headlights washed over a sign warning of steep grades and sharp turns ahead. The road curved into a forest. He glanced at the side mirror.

Koma sighed. "What a day, what a day," he said, still smiling. "If only Uncle called a few minutes earlier, it would've been a happier ending. This means war with the Dragon. Surely they'll be gunning for us all. We will need to take precautions. Change where we eat, get our dry cleaning done -- I won't be able to show my face at the Palace of the Sunfish until we settle our scores. No more packages. The magistrate who was blown to bits in Kyoto...that was the Dragon. The sneaky bastards love letter bombs. This is terrible."

Yes, yes, Nanashi thought Koma had it right. This was terrible. Then he glanced in the mirror and saw Mizo's headlights make a hard right onto an access road and vanish into the darkness. He tried to recall what lay down that road--an estuary, a canal, something on that order. A chill stole over him and he experienced a split second premonition of evil that caused him to swoon. The car lurched and Koma swore, not aware of the drama unfolding behind them.

What could it mean?

"Shit, we are definitely in trouble." Nanashi coasted onto the shoulder until bits of grit and gravel crunched under the Cadillac's wheels, then switched the hazard flashers on and smoked his cigarette. He fished out a flask of whiskey and had a sip while Koma stared at him incredulously. Nanashi observed a stream of headlights the mirror, daring to hope, but none belonged to Mizo's Honda.

Haru stuck his face over the front seats and said, "What is it? Why are we stopped? Give me some of that booze."

Nanashi gave him the booze and when Haru had drunk greedily, Nanashi handed the flask to Koma who also took a long, shuddering drink. Nanashi said, "The twins split."

"Split?" Koma's eyes were wild. He rolled down the window and twisted in his seat to look backward along the highway. "Where the hell are those clowns? How could they get lost? Idiots! Now is the time to stick together!"

"Not lost. Just gone." Nanashi rubbed his eyes.

"Dumbass. You should've said something."

"Oh, no," Haru said. "Those crazy bastards. I always knew something like this was bound to happen. The cowards have run away. Scurried into the night like rats."

Nanashi didn't think that was the case--the twins were stupid and stupidly fearless. Neither would think to flee the coming apocalypse until they were trapped in a cellar and being flayed alive by Dragon enforcers. He kept his peace, however.

"But wait." Koma slumped into his seat. "Those idiots don't run from a fight. Is it possible we've been betrayed? Did the Dragon get to them? We pay them like shit, that's for sure."

Haru snatched the flask and shook his head between gulps. "No way. The Dragon only wants them for fish bait. Even those two retards wouldn't be that dumb."

This was true. Once upon a time the twins had crossed the rival gang in such a spectacular fashion that there could be no rapprochement under any conceivable circumstance. The twins had gained their celebrated status as dreaded Heron enforcers after the legendary feat of storming a fortified stronghold and executing eight soldiers of the Dragon Syndicate who'd assembled to plot an attack on the Heron Clan. It was a slaughter of such magnitude (the soldiers were renowned assassins and all around tough guys) and conducted with such ruthlessness and audacity that the criminal underworld buzzed for months afterward. Uncle Nobukazu, the twins' patron, basked quite smugly in the afterglow. He was said to have visited the duo in their private hospital room (as they'd suffered serious injuries during their heroics), waiting upon them hand and foot with sweets, cigarettes, and liquor.

Yes, the Terrible Two managed to murder eight foes at a single go, however, the feat wasn't quite as heroic as the storytellers later made it out to be. For one thing, the rival gangsters had gathered in a shabby motel, not a fortress sanctum. For another, the Dragons hadn't assembled to assault the Herons, they'd been summoned by the syndicate elders to await orders for escorting a shipment of designer clothing they'd extorted a small corporation into selling them on the cheap. Nothing exotic or particularly important about the job, which was why all of the men involved were either foot soldiers or hard cases long past their prime. The Terrible Two got wind of the caper from a little creep on the periphery of the Dragon Syndicate, a shiner of shoes and fetcher of sake who'd taken a kick in the ribs from one of his betters and decided to get revenge. The creep happened to share a needle in a den with two likely friends and thus history was written.

As it happened, the twins had recently come into possession of ancient surplus military hardware including an AK-47 and a real live functioning flamethrower circa WWII. Neither of the goons had the foggiest clue regarding the care and operation of a pack of crayons much less a lethal antipersonnel device. Be that as it may, after gleaning the basic mechanics from a how-to internet video, the Terrible Two packed the flamethrower and some guns into a sports car Mizo jacked from behind a seedy tavern and away they went, both of them fidgeting from the coke they'd snorted that afternoon.

They spent half the evening locating the flophouse motel where their quarry lurked, then circled the joint a dozen times in an effort to scope the opposition. Jiki took a turn at the wheel and rear-ended another car and received a warning from the police. Lucky for him there was a major traffic accident across town and the distracted cops didn't run the plates on the stolen car or happen to glance in the backseat where deadly weapons were stacked in plain view.

Phase Two saw them creeping through a field of shrubbery and broken glass until they were huddled outside the roomful of over-the-hill yakuza. The Dragons were drunk and drugged up. Some slept, others sat around in their underwear, smoking grass, playing cards, and scratching flabby guts while cops and robbers shot each other on the television. Jiki and Mizo were not quite so foolish as to charge in, guns blasting, not quite so ferociously suicidal. In any event, Mizo was particularly intrigued to see what havoc he could wreak with his new toy, which he'd strapped to his back and primed for action.

The gang was oblivious to their impending doom, with the exception of one fellow sitting cross-legged on a bed next to the window. This gangster was so stoned he had no clue what to make of the wand slipping between the blinds, and actually cocked his head to peer down the nozzle right before Mizo squeezed the trigger.

The entire motel went up in flames. People, yakuza and innocent guests alike, shrieked and died as smoke boiled and the black sky was painted hellish hues of orange and red. The Terrible Two fled for the car, laughing and hooting in hyena joy, and all might've gone perfectly if Jiki, who drove because Mizo was still lugging the flamethrower, hadn't decided to cruise past the scene of the inferno to gloat over their victory. A Dragon enforcer staggered from the conflagration clad only in shorts--hair smoldering, face slagged from the intense heat--and unloaded his dual automatic pistols. Jiki panicked and floored the accelerator and the yakuza stood in the middle of the road with action hero aplomb, popping off a few final rounds at their disappearing taillights before he collapsed in a smoldering heap and died. Meanwhile, a bullet punched through the car's rear window and ricocheted from the tank on Mizo's back. He screamed in surprise and Jiki swerved all over, tires screeching, rubber burning, and somehow during the confusion the flamethrower got set off again and turned the car into a fireball Jiki promptly steered off the street and into a canal.

Satan apparently watches over his own because both men survived with minor burns, a few broken bones, and singed scalps. Hailed as heroes of the clan, only a handful of insiders ever knew the reality: The Terrible Two were a pair of craven, fucking morons. Famous fucking morons, now.

The Dragon Syndicate were not amused.

By the grace of iron-strong custom and venerable gangster tradition regarding truces were Jiki and Mizo kept from being summarily abducted and tortured and fed to the fishes. Sadly enough.

Nanishi said, "So much for the honor of ninkyō dantai," and laughed.

"What now?" Haru said in a thick voice. Amida moaned.

"We can't return to the office without the corpse." Koma had taken the cell phone from his pocket, but obviously lacked the courage to ring Uncle Yutaka with the current news. Things were likely tense around the gang clubhouse. "Okay, piss on it. Move over, I'm driving."

Koma and Nanashi traded places, although Koma didn't get moving right away. The four of them hunched for a while in the shadows, sporadically illuminated by the hazards and the flare of passing headlights. Nanashi shut his eyes and the black motes aligned like a Venus flytrap's teeth snapping together.

The ghost of Muzaki whispered, *There are those who claim that Time is a ring. I have found it to be a maze, and my own role that of the Minotaur. Rabbit, O rabbit. Welcome to the maze.*

* * *

One often falls in dreams. In this case, Nanashi had the sense of traveling at great speed, like a bullet shot through the heart of a void. His eyes opened and blackness resolved into light and sound. Music scratched from a vinyl record -- Black Betty by the venerable Ram Jams. Karaoke was quite popular with the yakuza and he'd learned all of the classics--Johnny Cash, Roger Miller, Led Zeppelin, The Beatles, The Clash, and dozens between. How many slobbering drunk renditions of "Green, Green Grass of Home" or "Folsom Prison Blues" had he delivered at yakuza bar haunts over the years? Lots and lots, was the answer.

The woman gave a short, stifled cry when she saw him in the middle of the hallway between the bathroom and bedroom. He would've said something to reassure her except for the inconvenient fact that his insides were on the verge of erupting. The vertigo felt similar to falling from an apartment window toward the upward rushing concrete.

This was the internationally renowned Susan Stucky in person, or in a dream that felt too close to reality for comfort. Lacking her customary pancake makeup and award-winning cinematography it had taken him a moment to place her. Shorter and thinner than he remembered, her blonde hair much darker and flung loose over her shoulder in a way she'd never worn it on celluloid; naked except for a pearl chain around her hips. Her flesh gleamed alabaster, pallid from shock or the soft low light that illuminated the passage.

Behind her lay a spacious living room decorated with wood and leather and stone. Moonlight dripped from the scalloped ceiling. A deep, steady growl emanated from the shadows, and a giant white and gray Akita swaggered into view, stiff-legged, hackles bunched. Heart-shaped tags jingled from its spiked collar as it slouched forward.

Nanashi smiled weakly at the brute and said, "Good doggie. Good boy." He said it in English. He liked dogs. He gripped the butt of his revolver anyway.

But neither the dog nor the woman were reacting to his presence. Muzaki stood in the doorway of the bathroom. The wrestler loomed larger than life, clothing shredded, blood coursing from a dozen vicious cuts and gashes. Part of his face was crushed into butcher meat. His left arm was gone, hacked away near the elbow to match the stump of his left leg. He smiled through a mouthful of pulverized teeth. Gore slopped from his lips. He winked his one good eye and toppled backward and the door flew shut.

Nanashi heard *Goodbye, goodbye, love,* as a rustle of dry leaves in his brain.

Now woman and dog finally registered Nanashi's presence. She patted the dog's head. Her expression lost its animating dismay and smoothed to ice. She inclined her chin toward the front of the house. "Company coming."

He almost asked who, and held his tongue. He knew exactly who. Word had traveled along the wire to Yokohama. Killers from the Heron would be en route. Possibly for murder, possibly for kidnapping. Either way it would be a routine clearing of accounts after the debacle with Muzaki, and lovely Susan Stucky wasn't long for the world. Her future consisted of ropes, knives, and a shallow grave. He found his cigarettes, lighted two. He crossed the floor and gave her one of the cigarettes, which she accepted wordlessly. She stared at him and her eyes were cold enough to burn. He studied the ceiling.

"You are remarkably composed," he said.

"So are you."

"Believe me. I'm shitting a brick."

"You must be a heavy."

"Oh yeah." He cracked his knuckles and loosened his tie.

She blew smoke. "Are you with me or against

me?" No lipstick, no inflection except impersonal curiosity. Her scent was coconut lotion and sex.

"That's a tough decision."

"What's the difficulty? I've got money if that's the hangup."

"I don't want your money. May not need it, either, depending on how this goes."

"It's going to go shittily if past is prologue. You're not stupid, not with that suit. What's the real problem?"

"I'm a lunatic or this is a dream."

"Oh? Transcendental meditation? A bad trip on some funky 'shrooms?"

He considered, shrugged. "Well, this scene doesn't seem possible. Maybe I'm a ghost. Maybe I'm an astral projection."

She casually reached up and slapped him. She'd had practice. "Nope, no silver cord. You're here for reals, as the kids say. Get your game face on, bitch."

He rubbed his mouth and smiled.

"Wes always said this moment would come. You're a Heron. I expected one of ours at least." Her gaze lingered on his open collar, the needlework. That she could read its fragment impressed him. "So, are you man or mouse? Friend or foe?"

The dizziness receded and Nanashi's legs steadied. His instinct took over now: balls retracted, adrenaline flowed, higher brain functions reduced to static. Fear made an ecstatic of him. "I'm a rabbit, apparently." His voice cracked. His gun was in his hand like magic. He moved past her into the living room, toward the main entrance, and gods it was a gorgeous home, opulent and cozy. He noted the decorative stones of a fountain, small busts of copper and bronze and jade, scarlet hangings and reed screens inlaid with onyx and gold calligraphy, bearskin rugs cast about haphazardly, and crossed polearms with tassels and pieces of samurai armor on stands and racks. So many wonderful things to kill with.

Muzaki had owned several such homes in Japan and others in the United States and Canada, and mistresses accompanied each. Truly a blessed man. Truly a cursed man.

Artificial fire flickered in the hearth. Rainbows of exotic fish shifted within tiered aquariums. These rainbows undulated across the woman and the dog as they silently watched him rush to drop the metallic drapes on the windows. The rainbow pattern splayed over the blinds, sealing off his glimpse of the front yard and the outer darkness that pressed just past the porch lights.

"Where are we?" he said.

"Near Yamagata," she said.

Yamagata lay many kilometers north of where he'd left his companions minutes ago. Before the blinds dropped he'd gotten an impression of big rocks and trees and assumed the property lay beyond the city limits. Several feet away the oak finish of a wet bar shone like true love and abutting it a cherry-panel turntable emitted its classic rock music. He opened a drawer and fixed himself a tall glass of Okuhida, tossed it back and poured another for himself and a fresh glass for the lady. She accepted the drink without comment. Confidence restored, he stared at her and downed his liquor. Neither of them blinked.

The dog whined uneasily. Its teeth were daggers.

Sweat trickled into the seams of Nanashi's forehead and seeped along his cheeks. He felt stirrings of power, the surging vitality of a gorilla, a shark, a tiger. Fire kindled in the center of him, his flesh tingled and tightened and his asshole contracted to a marble. The sweet-bitter tastes of adrenaline cut with vodka prickled his tongue. A ferocious recklessness built within him not unlike the approaching climax of a sex act. He yawned, not quite ready, not quite there, but close.

"Oh, I like you," she said without sounding as if she really did.

"Muzaki-san said the same." The player clunked and a new record began to spin. Hair of the Dog, by Nazareth. He threw back his head and laughed from the belly. A roar. He realized she'd been dancing in the nude to the classic rock of her homeland when he and the grotesque phantom of her husband intruded so dramatically. He'd seen her dance onscreen, an erotic Dance of the Seven Veils routine for her Mafioso husband that caused audiences and critics to salivate. The Academy tossed her an Oscar nomination as a reward.

A bell gonged, twice. The front door came off its hinges.

Nanashi knew the one in charge, a slim man with a shaved head and blond goatee by the name of Kada. Kada the Sadist, some muttered. Kada the Brave. Kada the Handsome. Kada, second son of the Chairman himself, so Kada the Favored. A playboy, even by yakuza standards. He'd tittered behind his hand when Nanashi lost a piece of his finger that fateful night long ago. Nanashi didn't recognize the other five. Dead men but for the formalities.

Kada dressed in white. His minions wore black suits and slick sunglasses despite the hour, each standing with stick-up-the-ass rigidity. A despised lieutenant and five brothers Nanashi had never met. Both facts made everything much easier. Not that it would've been particularly hard on him in the first place. The Heron Clan had always treated him more as a favored dog than beloved family. His contempt and fear and the pulsing vodka flames helped. The smoldering disdain in the actress's eyes helped even more.

Kada appraised the situation with the imperious demeanor of a visiting Daimyo, his own sunglasses held between thumb and forefinger, tapping against his thigh. He raised an eyebrow. "I am surprised to see you here, little brother."

"How many more are outside?" Nanashi said, bowing curtly; a dip that barely satisfied protocol but allowed him to keep his eyes on the Sadist.

"There were a couple of guys in the yard. We took care of them. The Dragons are punks. Has this bitch given you any trouble?"

"No. I meant how many more men do you have?"

The blond hesitated, studying the room more closely. He slipped on his shades. "Just us. I don't need an army to collect a woman."

Nanashi raised the gun and shot him in the face.

Who taught you to fight? Muzaki said. He and Nanashi were on a beach in the gray light of dawn. Surf packed the sand and glazed it with pebbles and dead starfish. A frigid breeze blew from the water. Muzaki wore an old, elegant suit. He was whole again. The shine in his eyes seemed too lustrous. The curve of his smile too wide. Who trained you to kill?

Nobody, Nanashi said. In the distance, amid the driftwood and the swirling ebb and flow of the tide lay a dark blot.

--Once it began, Nanashi committed to his art with the dispassion and precision of clockwork machinery. He was all gears turning and springs uncoiling as he half crouched, free hand at midsection level, poised in a claw, gun arm stabbing forward. He swung the revolver, swung his entire body with pendulum smoothness and drilled the pair flanking their fallen leader. Three bullets, three down, but he missed with the fourth, while the fifth only clipped a man's shoulder and the survivors dove for cover. Two had pistols and the last wielded a sawed-off shotgun--

They don't teach you to kill in the dojo. Not in modern times.

Nobody taught me.

You burst whole from Jupiter's aching skull. A prodigy. A shark.

One day I picked up a knife. Later, I picked up a gun. I was also pretty quick to learn to peddle a bike and quite handy with a tit. They kept walking without stretching their legs and the distant blot squirmed and grew.

Muzaki said, I was lost as a young man during a shipwreck, out there. I suppose you know the story. Ring announcers have told it for decades.

--the shotgun gave Nanashi anxiety. He decided to kill that enemy next. The Akita had the same idea. It pounced on the guy, jaws locking onto his abdomen, shaggy body wrenching side to side in a frenzy that went straight back to the days of caves and saber tooth cats. The shotgun boomed and guts unspooled everywhere--dog guts, man guts, a jet of commingled guts, a sluice of seared blood and viscera. The man fired again, screaming in terror and agony, then he stopped screaming and the dog stopped growling.

Shotgun guy was the one Nanashi had clipped and now he wondered if the slug had severed something important because the end came too quickly. Oh, but who was he to argue with the gods of death? A pall of smoke rolled over the room and Nazareth kept saying now somebody was messing with a sonofabitch. The house stank of burning hair, of burning blood, of scorched silk.

Crack, crack, crack went the popgun automatics accompanied by tiny spurts of flame from behind a potted plant and an overturned sofa where the yakuza had taken refuge. A bullet kicked loose carpeting near Nanashi's polished shoe. Another bullet burnt past his ear and pinged through the metal drapery. Nanashi flung the revolver and palmed the stiletto he kept under his armpit. The guy behind the sofa was on empty and Nanashi vaulted it, knelt and one! two! piston-fast, stabbed the gangster in the throat as he struggled to reload. The guy kept fumbling with the cartridge and swatting at the blood pouring down the front of his suit, until his movements were slow motion. Nanashi forgot him and kept going, scuttling on all fours toward the miniature banyan tree in its wicker pot and directly for the gangster ridiculously exposed as he cowered there. The gangster was a kid, hard and cruel, his face already nicked and scarred. The kid lined up the barrel of his nickel-plated automatic and uncapped however many rounds he had left as Nanashi floated toward him, moving with the rock and sway of a hominid torn from a primordial hunting ground and projected across time and space into that ruined living room--

I don't recognize this place, Nanashi said. The beach continued to unreel. The landscape warped and refracted black and white, a negative. The ocean was blinding white.

This is the Maze, Muzaki said. His face shimmered a dull ivory and suggested that while the wounds had sealed he remained a bloodless, shambling thing that should not be. What is that? He pointed toward the shivering black spot that drew ever closer.

Nanashi strained to see and when he did he understood that a heavy stone had been rolled aside to reveal a secret nest that should've remained hidden. He fell to his knees and began to shriek, pop-eyed and insane.

Muzaki said, Don't be afraid, my nameless friend. You've done well and I'm here. I'm here for you. I've always been.

--goon number six was too frightened to aim straight and his shots went wherever errant shots go and then Nanashi slammed a knee into his chin and there went teeth, tongue, a yolk of blood and spit. The kid sprawled and Nanashi kicked him in the neck and again in the base of the spine. Bone crunched and the kid became still.

Nanashi straightened and breathed hard. He wiped his face with his sleeve.

"Are you finished?" Susan Stucky hadn't moved from her position in the hallway. She dropped her cigarette butt and carefully negotiated the battlefield to the record player and yanked the cord out of the wall. A man who'd survived his horrible injuries groaned where he lay in the fetal position in a thickening pool of blood. Otherwise the house was quiet. The actress was alone at last, or so Nanashi surmised. Lost to her Hollywood cliques, the tabloids no longer bothered to mention her, an alien in alien land and doubly estranged by her own wealth, her princess-style investiture at Castle Muzaki. She went over and peered at the wounded man who stirred and raised his bloodied hand to her in supplication. She stepped back and gave Nanashi a look.

He retrieved his pistol and reloaded it without thinking; his mind sprinted ahead, calculating avenues of escape, vectors of pursuit, safe-houses, odds of prolonged survival. Violence, its preparation and aftermath, was his meditation. He didn't waste another bullet, simply hefted the fractured jade bust of some ancient dead god of the sea and smashed the gangster's skull with such force the man's glazed eyes started from their sockets and splashed against Nanashi's shoe. When Nanashi turned, he saw Susan Stucky kneeling by her dead dog and stroking its fur.

"All right," she said with dull satisfaction at the mess he'd made of her enemies. "These poor saps never stood a chance, huh? Good for us that they trusted you. You jumped across that line awfully quick."

There was a psychedelic moment where he relived every slashed throat, every gouged eye, every severed finger, every beating he'd administered purely upon orders from his Sworn Family for reasons he seldom understood. He'd once ripped a businessman's tongue free with pliers and fed it to him. He'd skinned a rival underboss alive with the edge of a trowel. He'd shoved a prostitute from a high rise roof knowing she was pregnant. And worse. Worse, always worse. He said, "Long time coming."

She straightened and regarded him. "You gangster boys are in a shooting war. The shit is going to hit the fan in a major way when news breaks of what happened to my beloved husband."

"We can't hang around." He snapped his fingers.

"Gather what you need and come on. Two minutes. I won't wait longer."

"Just bring the car around, rabbit." She mockingly snapped her fingers behind her head as she turned away.

He walked through the main door, keeping his stride brisk yet unhurried. The night air tasted of pine and mineral dampness. As he'd presumed, Kada lied--there were two compact cars parked at the foot of the broad flagstone steps. Two men in the lead car, a driver in the second. The two in front allowed him to approach within spitting distance before the passenger side door flew wide and raucous techno music blasted forth. Stupid kids.

Nanashi gave the emerging gangster a friendly wave and put two rounds into his chest, then ducked low and shot the driver through the open door. The other driver had the presence of mind to throw his car into reverse. Unfortunately for him, he banged into an ornate retaining wall and by the time he'd changed gears and hit the accelerator Nanashi tapped the window with the barrel of his revolver. The man shouted an obscenity or a prayer and then he died with a smoking hole in his cheek. Nanashi toppled the corpse into the driveway, swept aside the frosting of shattered glass and climbed behind the wheel and waited.

* * *

Smoke billowed from the house. Red fire twinkled and capered. She'd smashed a few bottles of alcohol and struck a match on her way through the door. "Watch that bitch burn," she said and buckled in. She'd put on a silver kimono and slippers. Her purse was some sort of designer plastic; bulky and glossy black. She chain-smoked gourmet cigarettes from an enamel case. He couldn't place them from their odor.

She gave clipped directions that sent them along secondary roads. It surprised him that the route carried them away from the city instead of closer. He drove at risky speeds, trying to keep his thoughts in sight. The slick, narrow blacktop entered mountainous forest-- white trees, white flashes of rock, white mist. The oni and the yokai were awake and traveling in parallel. Ghosts of hunger and vengeance cried the cry of night birds.

"There's a book about a woman whose husband randomly travels through time," she said. "It's a tearjerker. Sold a bajillion copies. That's what tearjerkers do."

"I haven't read it," he said.

"Are gangsters allowed to read chick lit?"

"Who's going to stop us?"

"Well, this situation with me and Wes is like that sci-fi scenario. Except not really. Also, the romance is dead. Everything is about death with Wes."

"Okay." As soon as the yakuza tracked her down, and soon it would likely be, she was definitely dead, although that wouldn't happen until she'd suffered enough to welcome annihilation.

"He did the paper trick, right? He always does the paper trick. I'm not sure whether that part is bullshit or not. I mean, the loony stuff about government mind control experiments is a red herring, but the pattern itself does pickle your brain all right. Doesn't require paper, though. He could draw it in the sand or wave his hands in the air. I kinda suspect he could even just use his voice to conjure the effect. What else did he say?"

Nanashi shrugged.

"There was a bit about time and mazes and blah, blah, blah."

"Blah, blah, blah," he said.

"Wes doesn't time travel. Time travel goes against Einstein, thus it's impossible. Something else very fucked up is going on. Not time travel, though. Did you kill him? Was it you personally?"

He shook his head. The engine purred. Wind snickered through the hole he'd made in the window.

"I want you to thank whoever did it."

"Send a postcard to the Yokohama office. The guys will appreciate the thought." He brushed his hair back; useless in the teeth of the wind. Eventually he sealed the hole with the palm of his hand.

"With Wesley's death, I am free."

He grunted.

"I was his slave. That was the price to pay for bringing me back from the underworld. He's King Pluto, our man Wes."

"Yeah? Are you certain he's not Polyphemus?"

"Don't you dig, killer? All the myths are the same. Geography just changes how we explain the horrors." She lighted yet another cigarette and smiled a tight, bitter smile. "You'll figure it out, bad boy. Act Two. Me, I'm beating feet."

"Where am I taking you, huh?"

"It would be meaningless to say. Fear not -- we're almost there."

You slaughtered your brothers. O woe unto thee! Nanashi could've tricked himself into hearing that whisper from Muzaki's lips instead of the pit of his own subconscious. *Slaughtered sworn brothers for what? This sharp-tongued gaijin with nice legs? Guilt? Your fear of something larger than yourself?* Yes, that last thing felt right. There was his motive. He'd become enmeshed in the action of powerful forces, a leaf in the flood.

"Okay," he said. "I am at your service."

She laughed and it wasn't the melodic timbre of her silver screen personae. This was swift, dark water over rocks, the quick bark of a crow. "Not mine, killer. You belong to a real sonofabitch." She laughed again. "There, turn there. That's my exit, stage left."

He parked in a leaf-strewn lot near a picnic table and a drinking fountain. A small placard indicated it might be a park or preserve -- the lettering was illegible and focusing upon it made his head ache.

Susan Stucky finished her cigarette. She opened her door and climbed out, pausing to lean back in and study him. In the dimness her expression was inscrutable. "Your boys are going to kill you?"

"If they find out that I helped you. Yes."

"You going to tell them?"

He shrugged.

"The macho honor bit," she said.

"Yeah."

"The Dragon?"

"Yeah." He smiled. "Nobody likes me."

She smiled back. "Okay, rabbit. Thanks."

"Wait."

"What?"

"Where will you go? This is a forest."

"You're very observant. Maybe in the next life you should be a detective." She slammed the door and walked in front of the car and followed the headlight beams. Her kimono shone like the moths milling around her pale hair. She vanished into the woodwork.

Nanashi smoked a cigarette while the engine idled. He sighed and got out and went after her. The slender trees were slick with dew. Fog dampened the rasp of his breath, his shoes scrabbling among roots and leaves. Illumination from the headlights quickly faded and he felt his way through opaline murk. Ahead, a bluish light infiltrated the forest. Shadows leaped around him as limbs creaked with a puff of wind.

Bushes rustled nearby and the Akita ghosted along, its white fur gone blue as an ice floe. Its eye flickered. Guts trailed from a fist-sized hole where the shotgun slug had torn through. Man and dog regarded one another in passing.

"The hell is this?" Nanashi said in wonderment. He almost expected Muzaki to mutter the answer. *Hell? Oh, yes, rabbit.*

The trees thinned and he caught glimpses of the born again dog. Once he could've sworn a woman's voice echoed from the distance. He scrambled down a steep embankment, grasping exposed roots to keep from pitching onto his face. At the bottom was a gully and a fast-moving stream. The water flowed shin deep and cold enough to shock his feet numb. He trudged downstream as the light intensified and set the cloying mist ablaze and forced him to shield his eyes.

The gully widened into a field of short, damp grass. The moon seethed through a low cloudbank, spotlighting a cherry blossom tree in a shaft of blue fire. The tree reared in stately menace where the water cut a delta around its gnarled bole. Empty suits and shoes dangled from the branches. Pieces of jewelry glimmered in knotholes. Thunder rumbled. His mind became so full it blankly mirrored the blue moon and struck him dumb, pinned him to the spot. The moon's eyelid peeled back and crimson radiance stabbed forth. Where the red light touched, grand black trees silently erupted from the grass like a child's popup book and from each tree depended the sinister fruit of empty clothing. Chimes tinkled and sang.

A dog howled, or a god. Nanashi ran, slipping and splashing along the ravine, making for the car. He rose and fell and rose again to flee onward. Blue haze before him shivered as it was eaten by the red ray of the moon. One sidelong glance revealed a figure keeping pace, a stumbling, screaming lunatic who much resembled himself, and there were others at intervals between the skinny poplars and pines. Each of them rising, falling, rising. At his back the dog's howl deepened to a roar and the roar became a vast ripping sound as of a pavilion torn asunder in a hurricane.

He began to fly.

* * *

Dawn refused to break.

Nanashi drove the stolen car *like* it was stolen, drove with the abandon of a dead man. He ignored the scenery and stared directly ahead, afraid to blink lest he find himself catapulted through time and space via the pattern imprinted within his eyelids. He didn't entertain conscious thought. He focused on the pavement lines, focused on the rhythm of shifting, of pressing the pedal to the floorboard.

It should've been light when he finally returned to the mountain lodge, but was not. The staff stared at him. Their terror was the terror of peasants at the mercy of vengeful samurai in times of war. His immaculate hair was disheveled and wild as a bushman's, his fine clothes spattered in mud and torn at the seams. Dirt and blood ingrained his fingernails. He pointed his revolver at the innkeeper and asked if he'd seen Koma or the others. The Innkeeper shook his head frantically and when Nanashi cocked the hammer the man fell to his knees and blubbered while his wife chanted a prayer and the gaggle of serving boys wrung their hands and moaned.

Nanashi put the gun away. What had he expected to find? He searched the lodge proper, knowing the act was useless, and next he investigated the cottages and the sweltering cave with its hot springs. All was locked tight and dripping silence. None of the gang had sneaked back for an emergency rendezvous. He should square his shoulders and head for the city, present himself before his Sworn Father and accept judgment. Either that, or flee the country forever. Yuki would quit her job and run away with him to a new life in America, somewhere the long arm of the clan couldn't reach. Problem was, the yakuza could reach anywhere. Such was the awful beauty of that particular monster. As for sweet Yuki... Yuki had family and friends, roots. She'd never consent to a fugitive life with her much older lover, a man of no status and bleak prospects.

Head down, he started the car and drove away, hands and feet making the necessary adjustments while his mind dissolved into itself. He was afraid and exhausted. There wasn't much else. Upon reaching the highway junction he steered south. His hands made the decision. Tears streamed down his cheeks. He gritted his teeth and clenched the leather of the steering wheel in a death grip.

Along the route to the pit where the Heron gang had done its murderous deed he stopped once to fill the tank. The station was deserted but for his car. Twilight smoldered at the periphery, held at bay by the plastic glow of the station lamps. He looked for signs in the contours of clouds, the constellations of dirt and debris that swirled across the pavement. Compelled by terrible inspiration, he finally dared to shut his eyes. When he opened them the tank had filled and a tiny woman smiled at him from the tiny screen on the pump.

Onward, he toiled.

Muzaki awaited him at the rim of the pit. He crawled forth over the lip in a parody of birth--first his clutching hands, then his head and torso, all of him moving at strange angles until he straightened to his full height. The wrestler appeared unscathed, albeit slightly pallid. He wore a white robe that gathered the frail light like the filament of a bulb. He got into the front passenger seat.

Nanashi swallowed hard. "Where do we go from here?"

"That depends on whether you saved her."

Nanashi remained silent. Muzaki nodded and a small, odd smile tugged at the corners of his blue lips. He pointed north with a hand that shone queerly alabaster.

Nanashi drove north. Kilometers rolled past. Dials and gauges reset themselves to their starting positions, but the car zoomed smoothly along the endless highway. He said, "I had a vision of Hell."

"Hell is just another neighborhood."

"I have tried to convince myself that this is a nightmare."

"Awake or dreaming, there's no appreciable distinction."

"Who are you? Are you even the man I watched on television all those years ago? Was there ever such a man?"

"I am a cursed, malignant brute. I cast a black aura. Other deserving souls, damned souls, in other words, sometimes catch in its hooks like fish in a dragnet."

There was nothing to say. They flew more kilometers through the changing gloom until Muzaki said, "We exist in a universe of miracles and curses. The shipwreck during my childhood was both. Those of us who survived the waves and the rocks and the sharks, were stranded upon an island. The island was barren. There was nothing to eat except for one another. So it went and madness followed. On the forty-ninth day, rescuers came. Pale Ones, terrible to behold. They brought me and a couple of others away from the island. The bones of the rest were left for the seagulls to pick."

Nanashi saw the child Muzaki lifted from the dirt by inhumanly gracile hands and borne across dark waters upon a gasp of wind. He beheld a crimson and purple mist, and through the mist the flint-sharp spikes of black cliffs streaked in white. He beheld towers, slender and jagged and cruel and the folk within them must also have been of a kind. An island of skulls and weeping shadows, haunted strains of melancholy tunes fluting through abandoned bones. A necropolis sanctuary. Nothing living could enter. Nothing human could enter. Yet there Muzaki had lived. There Muzaki had supped. There Muzaki had grown ever stronger with the passing cycles of time and tide.

Nanashi trembled and bit his tongue just to feel the pain and be reassured that he yet dwelt among the living.

Muzaki gestured and they took a spur that angled toward the sea. Nanashi spotted Koma's Cadillac nosed into the ditch. Its doors were sprung. Bullet holes stitched the cobalt paint. The windows were blasted out. Glass and blood made a tapestry of the plush interior. The corpses were disfigured beyond recognition. Fistfuls of shell casings from automatic rifles glinted upon the ground. Nanashi wondered who'd betrayed his brothers to the Dragon; a passing thought not unlike a stray cloud floating across the subterranean sky.

Muzaki read his mind. "Were the gracious Innkeeper and his wife afraid to see you? Afraid as if you'd returned from the grave?"

"Yeah."

"Ah. I regret to inform you that those inestimable persons have dealt family secrets to your foes for many, many years. We should continue, eh?"

"I have seen enough."

"It's not *enough* until you've seen everything. Hurry!"

A bit farther the road branched and branched again and they came to a seawall. Jiki and Mizo's Honda was parked in an otherwise empty lot near a metal pavilion that had toppled. No sign of the Terrible Two.

Nanashi pulled alongside the Honda and exited. His clothes were whipped by a breeze that came hard and cold, strong with salt and kelp stench and bits of sand. His hair fell across his face. Muzaki grasped his elbow and guided him down the wooden ramp to the beach.

"What are you?" Nanashi said.

"An eater of carrion."

"Will you tell me something? I saved your wife. I kept my bargain."

"I do not recall any bargain."

"Tell me something. Please."

"I've told you of mazes and curses and damned souls. Yet you speak of nightmares and lunacy. I tell you that the dead and the undead may travel freely within the static maze of reality, indeed, I have shown you the truth of the maze. You choose blindness, deafness. Human primates do so treasure their ignorance. Would that I could reclaim my own innocence of the howling wilderness that goes on forever."

"None of this makes sense," Nanashi said.

"Don't you feel how cold my hand is, Nanashi?"

Nanashi did not answer.

"If your future happiness depends upon my revelations, then you are doomed to an existence of abject misery." Muzaki's odd smile spread across his broad features, warping them into something alien. "There are planets and stars and mountains and forests. There are great, hungry fishes in the sea. There is you and I, Hell and Not Hell. There is the simple fact that knowing doesn't equal enlightenment. You are a bit of cotton dipped in the blood of the cosmos. That which is seen seeps inside and stains you. You have been stained, Nanashi-san. But, there is always more. Corruption is never finished with us."

Pieces of skeletal driftwood and seashells crunched underfoot. The tide rolled in, green and black and thunderous. Farther along the shore was the dark spot Nanashi half-recalled from the phantasms he'd suffered while battling to protect the gaijin woman back at the house. As the true nature of the aberration crystallized in his mind, he gave a hoarse cry and threw himself prostrate and refused to move. Muzaki tenderly leaned down and clutched a fistful of hair and effortlessly dragged him over the hard-packed sand and toward the crashing waves.

Nanashi struggled like a baby. Vertigo returned with a vengeance. Sea and sky folded around them in origami fashion and drew them forward at tremendous velocity. A rocky isle materialized from the void and then Nanashi was cast sprawling. He spat dirt. Pebbles gouged his elbows and knees. Nothing of the world existed beyond the beach shelf and surrounding rocks except for the sea and the clouds that reflected the sea.

Jiki and Mizo's Honda sat on a tilt, buried to the axles, where the beach curved. It had changed from how it had appeared in the parking lot. Blotchy handprints marred the window glass, doors, and hood.

Koma and his gangsters had dragged a mangled corpse nearby to a depression among the roots of a driftwood stump gone gray with age. The corpse bore a terrible resemblance to Muzaki. The men squatted in their ragged suits, but for Jiki and Mizo who'd stripped naked and now languished in the unnatural light. Their flesh gleamed as gray as the driftwood, and they preened, supremely unaffected by the chill wind or the salty spray that occasionally lashed them. The wretched creatures savaged the corpse, clawing into crevices and cavities for the choicest morsels. Koma, his fine jacket saturated to a deep maroon, snapped a rib free and wrapped his pointed tongue around it and slurped.

The gang hesitated when they spied Nanashi, chunks of meat held close to their gaping jaws. Each regarded him with the bright-placidity of lazing crocodiles. Muzaki snarled, a bestial utterance fit to freeze a man's heart, and the unholy things cowered and grinned.

"*Brother,*" croaked Amida, ashen visage smeared in fresh gore, collar undone. His left arm dangled. He didn't seem to mind. His eyes were pure black, his sneer sharp and ravenous.

"*Brother!*" said the rest, happy.

Muzaki said, "Lo, the feast of the ghouls. This rock is the banquet table of their ilk and I, the master of ceremonies. I live, die, am consumed, and reborn in the sticky, rancid cycle that governs all matter." His flesh too had darkened to the sickly gray of spoilage and antiquity. His eyes were reptilian and ebon. He breathed out fumes of kelp and sickness and decay. "Oh, rabbit. I've lived a thousand lives, but always it comes to this. For this is the reality behind my façade."

When at last he could speak, Nanashi said, "Why did you have me protect the woman?"

"In my way I loved her."

"Such a monster as yourself can know love?"

"Yes. It is the most exquisite corruption, the greatest perversion dreamt of by the forces of darkness. There can be no curse without love."

The ghouls tittered in chorus and dug into the wrestler's old, abandoned meat.

Muzaki gestured languidly, imperiously, and

several meters offshore the water gathered itself and bulged outward in a slick green dome. An iris slowly widened, revealing a tunnel that corkscrewed who knew where. He said, "Man with No Name, you are the sole living being on this island. Your old life is burned to ash. There are two paths remaining. Here among the ghouls and rebirth into the unlife. Or, out there and the unknown. You must choose."

Nanashi gazed first at the tunnel, then at the gory repast of his undead brothers. He groaned and wept. He drew the revolver and slid the barrel into his mouth. For an age he struggled to squeeze the trigger. Defeated, he dropped the gun and stood.

"Go," Muzaki said. "This is not for you."

For several moments Nanashi swayed, his sight turned inward. Abruptly he bent and snatched the revolver. Six bullets. Six targets. Perhaps it was fate. Perhaps it was fate mocking him. "This place isn't for anyone." He began to fire.

* * *

Nanashi threw the gun into the sea. He followed its arc. Hitching, halting, almost drunken, his feet carried him from the scene of slaughter and into the infinite mystery.

 Laird Barron spent his early years in Alaska, where he raced the Iditarod three times during the early 1990s——and worked in the fishing and construction industries. He is the author of several books, including *The Croning, The Imago Sequence, Occultation, The Light Is the Darkness,* and *The Beautiful Thing That Awaits Us All.* His work has also appeared in many magazines and anthologies. An expatriate Alaskan, Barron currently resides in upstate New York.

Bonus Material

Blood
&
Stardust

Three years later, as I hike my skirt to urinate in a dark alley in the slums of Kolkata, my arms are grasped from behind. The Doctor whispers, "So, we meet again." His face was ruined in the explosion—its severe, patrician mold is melted and crudely reformed as if an idiot child had gotten his or her stubby fingers on God's modeling clay. I can't see it from my disadvantaged perspective, but that's not necessary. I've been following him and Pelt around since our original falling out.

Speaking of the Devil...Pelt slips from the shadows and drives his favorite dirk first through my belly, then, after he smirks at the blood splattering onto our shoes, my heart. He grins as he twists the blade like he's winding a watch.

"—and this time the advantage is mine." I laugh with pure malice, and die.

* * *

Storms unnerve me. I hate thunder and lightning—it makes me jumpy, even in the Hammer Films I watch nearly every evening. Regardless the patent cheesiness, storms awaken my primitive dread. Considering the circumstances of my birth, that makes sense. Fear of the mother of elements is hardwired into me.

My nerves weren't always so frayed; once, I was too dull to fear anything but the Master's voice and his lash. I was incurious until my fifth or sixth birthday and thick as a brick physically and intellectually. Anymore, I read anything that doesn't have the covers glued shut. I devour talk radio and Oprah. Consequently, my neuroses have spread like weeds. Am I getting fat? Yes, I've got the squat frame of a Bulgarian power lifter, but at least my moles and wens usually distract the eye from my bulging trapeziuses and hairy arms.

I also dislike the dark, and wind, and being trussed hand and foot and left hanging in a closet. Dr. Kob used to give me the last as punishment; still does it now and again, needed or not, as a reminder. Perspective is extremely important in the Kob house. The whole situation is rather pathetic, because chief among his eccentric proclivities, he's an amateur storm chaser. Tornadoes and cyclones don't interest him so much as lightning and its capacity for destruction and death. Up until his recent deteriorating health, we'd bundle into the van and cruise along the coast during storm season and shoot video, and perform field tests of his arcane equipment. Happily, those days seem to be gone, and none too soon. It's rumored my predecessor, daughter *numero_uno*, was blown to smithereens, and her ashes scattered upon the tides, during one of those summer outings.

* * *

Time has come for action.

My birthday was Saturday. I'm thirty, a nice round number. By thirty, a girl should have career aspirations, picked out a man, that sort of thing. I stuck the white candle of death in a cupcake, said my prayers, and ate the damned thing with all the joy of a Catholic choking down a supersized holy wafer. Then I doused my sorrows with a bottle of Glenfiddich and watched a rerun of the late night creature-feature.

I've decided to record my deepest thoughts, although I'm young to be scribing even this outline of a memoir. Some bits I've written in spiral notebooks with ponies and unicorns on the cover.

* * *

We live in a big Gothic mansion on a hill outside of Olympia. We being Dr. Kob, Pelt, and me. Pelt came to the U.S. with the Master. The old troll doesn't talk much, preferring to hole up in his backyard tree house and drink Wild Turkey and sharpen his many, many knives. I call him Uncle, although so far as I know he's no more my uncle than the good Doctor is my father.

Dr. Kob's workshop is the converted attic in the East Wing. He's got a lordly view of everything from

Olympia to Mt. Rainier. When he's in his cups, he refers to the people in the city as *villagers*. That's exactly how he says it—with a diabolical sneer. I think he reminisces about the Motherland more than he should. His skeletons are banging on the closet door. He just keeps jamming in new ones. I wager it'll bite him in the ass one of these fine days.

The housekeeper, chef, and handyman stay in bungalows in the long shadows of the forest on the edge of the property. The gardener and his helpers commute daily. They tend the arboretum and the vast grounds. Yet despite their indefatigable efforts to chop back the vines, the brambles, and the weeds, the estate always seems overgrown. It looks a lot like the thicket around Sleeping Beauty's castle in the classic cartoons. Some rooms in the mansion leak during rainstorms. Like the grounds crew, our handyman and his boys can't replace rotten shingles and broken windows fast enough to stay ahead of entropy that's been gathering mass since 1845. There's not enough plaster or paint in the world to cover every blister and sore blighting this once great house.

But Dr. Kob doesn't care about such trivialities. He's obsessed with his research, his experiments. Best of all, there are catacombs beneath the cellars; an extensive maze chock full of bones. Beats digging up corpses at the graveyard in the dead of night, although he waxes nostalgic about those youthful excursions.

I'm careful in my comings and goings despite the fact Dr. Kob crushes the servants under his thumb and virtually saps their will to live. He imported most of them from places like Romania and Yugoslavia. They've united in tight jawed dourness and palpable resentment. None speak English. They're paid to look the other way, to keep their mouths shut. They know what's good for them.

I worry anyway. I'm a busy bee, fetching and toting for the Master; coming and going, sneaking and skulking at all hours. Capturing live subjects is dangerous, especially when you're as conspicuous as I am. There can be complications. Once, I brought home three kids I'd caught smoking dope in the park. The chloroform wore off one of them, and when I popped the trunk he jumped out and ran into the woods, screaming bloody murder. Luckily, Pelt was sober enough to function, for a change, and he unleashed a pair of wolfhounds from the kennel. Mean ones. We tracked the boy down before he made it to a road. The little sucker might've escaped if I hadn't cuffed his hands behind his back.

* * *

In unrelated events:

A circus rolled through town one week in the fall; in its wake, consternation and dismay due to a murder most foul. An article in the *Olympian* documents the spectacular and mysterious demise of Niall the Barker. The paper smoothes over the rough edges, skips most of the gruesome facts. The reporters in the know talked to the cops who know this: While hapless Niall lay upon his cot in a drunken stupor, some evil doer shoved a heavy duty industrial strength cattle prod up his ass and pressed the button. His internal organs liquefied. A blowhole opened in the crown of his skull, and shit, guts, and brains bubbled forth like lava from a kid's volcano exhibit at a science fair. His muscles and skin hardened and were branded with the most curious Lichtenburg Flowers.

Sometimes I go back and watch it again, just to savor the moment.

* * *

Dr. Kob requires that we take supper together on Fridays. We sit at opposite ends of a long, Medieval-style table in the dining hall. The hall is gloomy and dusty and decorated in a fashion similar to Dracula's castle in the Bela Lugosi, Christopher Lee films. God, how I adore Christopher Lee, especially the young, B-movie incarnation. His soliloquy to carnal delights in *The Wicker Man* stands my hair on end. Dr. Kob doesn't know anything about cinema or actors. He says there's no television where he comes from, no theatre. That's likely an exaggeration—the Master is fond of hyperbole. Read a few of his interviews in the *Daily O* and you'll see what I mean.

Dr. Kob's father was an eminent scientist until some scandal swept him and his family into the shadows. After his expulsion from whatever prominent university, Kob Sr. conducted his research in the confines of home sweet home. I think of the dungeons and oubliettes in those ancient European keeps and feel a twinge of pity for the peasants moiling in the fields beneath the Kob estate. Ripe fruit, the lot of them.

Snooping about the Master's quarters, I unearth a musty album full of antiquated photographs of Dr. Kob and various friends and relatives. Many feature the redoubtable Pelt. Has the hunter always been Kob's henchman? Perhaps they are fraternity brothers or blood cousins. Today the good Doctor bears a strong likeness to Boris Karloff, which is also pretty much how he looks in his baby pictures.

On the other hand, the Pelt I know scarcely resembles the man posing with a pack of hounds, his curls long and golden, his bloodthirsty grin as sweet and guileless as Saint Michael's own. What a heartbreaker (and likely serial killer) he was! One of the pictures is dated 1960. Now, he slumps over his plate and goblet. His hooked nose, his sallow cheeks are gnarled as plastic that's been melted and fused. Oh, and he's pot-bellied and bald as a tumor. It's all very sad—he's like a caricature of a Grimm Brothers' illustration. Maybe this is how Rumpelstiltskin ended his days.

"Mary had a little lamb," Dr. Kob says, and titters as he downs another glass of port. That Mary business annoys me more than he can imagine. He doesn't realize I caught on to his stupid inside joke and its antecedent years ago. *I read_classical_literature_too,_you pompous_ass*. I've Melville, Dickens, and Chaucer in the bedside cupboard. And Shelley, that bitch. On the other hand, perhaps I should be grateful. He could've named me Victor or Igor.

"—Mary had a little lamb—"

"—then she had a little mutton," Pelt says in an accent so thick you'd need one of his pig-stickers to cut it. I don't think Pelt likes me, our occasional drunken coupling notwithstanding. It's not exactly easy to find a good screw in this pit. I wonder if Dr. Kob knows about Pelt and me. The Old Man is cagey—I wouldn't be surprised if Pelt reported the results of our trysts as part of some twisted experiment like the Apted documentaries that appear on PBS every seven years.

Man, I'd love to get in front of a camera and monologue about some of the shit I've seen. Yeah, there's a frustrated actor in here. A frustrated nymphomaniac as well—sorry Pelt.

* * *

Midday now and I taste the ozone; my joints ache. From the parapet of the attic tower I can see way out across the water to where the horizon has shifted into black. It's coming on fast, that rolling hell.

The trees start to shake. Leaves come loose and flutter past my face. This is going to be a hummer. My hair is already frizzing. High elevations are bad places to be at times such as these. This particular roof is even worse than most because of all the lightning rods. Well, they aren't exactly lightning rods in the traditional sense. They serve other uses, primarily transferring electricity to the Doctor's lab equipment. Like a good gopher, I've come to make certain everything is shipshape—the array is rather delicate and must be aligned precisely. There's nothing more complicated about the job than jiggling a television antenna until the picture clears, but it has to be right or all hell might break loose.

I make the adjustments and then retreat inside and head for the kitchen. One of the chef's minions, a cook named Helga, fixes me cocoa and marshmallows. I'm sitting on one of the high stools, swinging my feet and sipping my hot chocolate when Dr. Kob comes around the corner, his usually slicked hair in disarray, his tie loose and shirt untucked.

"Mary," he says. "You double checked the array, I presume?" He scarcely acknowledges my answer; his mind is already three jumps ahead, and besides, my loyalty is unquestioned. "One of my specimens expired last night—but all is not lost. My revivification project awaits!"

"Remember not to talk on the phone during the storm," I say. "I just saw an account of a woman who was fried doing dishes. Ball lightning exploded from the sink and set her on fire. It traveled through the pipes."

Dr. Kob stares at me, his beady eyes narrowed. He rubs his temples as if experiencing a migraine. "You're watching the talk shows again. You know how I frown upon that, my dear. Less daydreaming, more physical exertion. Remind me to have Pelt assign you additional duties. Idle hands and all that."

"Sure, gimme a pitchfork and I'll swamp out the stables."

"Never mention pitchforks again!"

"Or torches."

"Out! Before I lose patience for your belligerence. And tomorrow, take the rod into our lovely village for quality assurance testing. I've altered the design. It possesses more jolt than ever."

"As you command," I say sweetly. After he wanders off, I chew my cup and swallow it piece by piece. It kind of frightens me that my Pavlovian dread of the Doctor has ebbed, replaced by an abiding irritation. This is very dangerous. He's a middle-aged megalomaniacal child—an *L' enfant Terrible*. We know what rotten children do with their toys, right?

He gave me a puppy, once. I loved her, and often imagined how she had crept into the caves of my ancestors to escape the cold and the dark. I accidentally broke the puppy's neck. It's probably a good thing he didn't hand me the little brother I always wanted.

* * *

Some people mow the lawn, others take out the garbage, or walk the pooch. Among similar menial tasks, I kidnap and kill whomever the Doctor says to kidnap or kill. I enjoyed it during my formative years. My rudimentary self was a glutton for the endorphin rush, the ecstasy of primal release. As my brain evolved, I developed, if not a conscience or morals, at least the semblance of ethics. The glamour has faded, alas, and now this too bores me to tears. Frankly, it's about as stimulating as tearing the limbs off dolls.

Usually I do the deed with this device Dr. Kob invented that's something on the order of an unimaginably powerful cattle prod. This prod is capable of emitting a charge much greater than the lethally electrified fences one might encounter surrounding a top secret military installation. It fits in my coat pocket and telescopes with the flick of my wrist, like those baton whips cops use to pacify rowdy protesters.

There are two basic methods of killing with the rod. (Dr. Kob encourages ample experimentation.) I jumped out of a hedge and zapped the last one, a banker in a suit and tie, from a distance of six paces. He shuddered and dropped in his tracks. Sometimes the energy exits from the temple or forehead and leaves a small hole like a bullet wound. I prefer to discharge from beyond arm's reach as a safety precaution, but it's not always feasible.

The second method is rather awful. The rod is thick at the base and gradually tapers to a point the diameter of a darning needle. A few weeks back I ministered to those two pole dancers who made such a sensation when the cops discovered them. And hell no, that particular job didn't bother me a whit. I'm not altogether fond of the pretty ones, and when they're haughty little bitch queens to boot…well, I consider it justice served. Anyway, their housemate walked in on the proceedings. I recognized him as a bouncer from the club where the girls worked—a powerfully built guy tattooed front and back, head to toe chains and piercings, and yellow, piggy eyes that burned with a love of violence. He almost got his hands on me before I stabbed him in the chest with the rod and dialed up the juice. The force hurled him end over end into the wall, where he sprawled, limbs flailing *grand mal* style. His eyes sizzled like egg yolks and sucked into his skull; his teeth shattered, his hair ignited, and all that miscellaneous metal reduced to slag as his skin charred and peeled. I'm no weak sister, but the greasy smoke, its stench, always gets me. I ran to the window and puked into a flower box. Then I got the hell out.

Dr. Kob wanted to hear everything, of course.

* * *

My lifelong fantasy about running away with the circus isn't likely to pan out. I'm okay with that. I buy tickets when a show's in town and make excuses to disappear for a few hours. Dr. Kob took me once when I was a child; for a while, he had this fascination with pretending I was his little girl. We went a lot of places during that happy period—picnics on the beach, the carnival, ice skating at the mall, and similarly nutty stuff. Nutty, because it was so damned out of character for the Doctor.

The circus is what sticks in my mind and I've continued to go long after the Doctor lost all interest in passing me off as his ugly daughter. I've even convinced Pelt to come along a couple of times, but not since he got into a row with a gang of carnies and cut off three fingers of one poor bastard. Pelt's an unpleasant drunk, to say the least.

A couple of weeks before my birthday, I'm scanning the paper and spot an advertisement for the impending arrival of the Banning Traveling Circus. Of such trivial things is treachery made....

This is a minor show, no Ringling Brothers extravaganza by any stretch, but it has elephants and trapeze artists and shiny women in leotards. One of the shiny women has long hair done in a single braid. A man dangles by his knees from the high swing, her hair clamped in his teeth as she spins below him with such velocity her limbs merge with her torso. The clowns zoom into the ring in their clown car, and the dancing bear wobbles in on his unicycle. Hijinks ensue. I clap, unable to contain my glee. It's all so damned simple I could cry.

After the main show I wander the grounds, a paper cup of beer in hand, a blob of pink cotton candy in the other. I resist the urge to visit the freak tent, and always fail. It's usually lame, and this collection is weaker than most. Crocodile boy has a serious overbite, and that's it. He's from Georgia and works as a hairdresser in the offseason. No two headed babies, no wolf men. The bearded lady is rather impressive, though. She's a brawny, Bavarian lass named Lila, who'd fit right in with the mansion staff. Her beard isn't particularly thick, yet it's immaculate and descends to her navel. Its point is waxed and gives her a sort of Mandarin vibe. She has the softest, greenest eyes.

She does her thing and it's getting dark, so the crowds trickle back to the parking lot under the pall of burnt kettle corn. Lila, Edna the tattooed lady, and I are talking and they invite me to the "after the show get-together"; a bunch of them always do. They gather under some tarps pitched between their trailers and wagons. I meet Cleo the strongman (who's definitely over the hill and suffering from chronic asthma), and Buddy Lemon and his wife Sri Lanka, the trapeze artists, and Armand, the guy who trains the lions and elephants, although I'm informed he sucks at both by Lila who whispers that two of the lions have mauled people and Dino stomped on a carnie, all in the last three months. Judging from how fast Armand guzzles a bottle of corn mash, I suspect she may be on to something.

They're a sweet bunch, raw and melancholy. As always, there's got to be one asshole in the crowd, though. A barker named Niall. A pigeon-chested guy with a pencil moustache and a waist like a fashion model. His crappy yellow and white striped suit is cut a size too small, even for him. He makes a snide remark about my "swarthy, and exceptionally stout" personage in a smarmy English accent. He tells Cleo to "watch out, mate, she appears as if she could beat you out of a job." I'm relieved and grateful when Lila glares and he slinks off to his quarters.

As the group drifts apart, Lila grabs my arm and says to come with her back to the trailer. I'm privately questioning the wisdom of this, because I've never had another woman come on to me before, and more importantly, there's the Doctor to consider. He keeps strange hours. There's no telling what mood he's in. I might be punished for leaving the house without permission. But I'm in a perverse mood so I follow her.

We're surrounded by farmland. It's extra dark on account of it being a moonless night, which Lila tells me is perfect for stargazing. She says the constellation she's been monitoring is tricky to capture due to its distance. Light pollution only adds to the degree of difficulty. She spends a few minutes adjusting the rig and muttering to herself, and I steady her elbow as she sways on unsteady legs.

Finally, she says, "Okay, all right, here we go. I'm getting damned good at this -- you have no idea how hard it is to nail down the Serpens galaxy." She guides my eye to the viewfinder and makes adjustments as I describe what I see, which at first isn't much but black space punctuated by random lights.

Then, "Oh. It's...beautiful." And it *is* beautiful, an impossibly remote field of stars veiled in clouds of dust and gas, and at its heart, a wavering flame that illuminates from the inside out, like fire shining through a smoky glass. I know it's old, old. Older even than my ancestors who scrabbled and clawed in the earliest days on this rock.

"Have you used a telescope before?"

"No," I say, slightly embarrassed that Dr. Kob often visits the Deer Mountain Observatory just a few miles from our house and yet I've never once asked to tag along.

"Don't blink," she says. "Like my Pa used to say, 'you gotta hold your jaw just right' when he taught me how to fire his deer gun. You blink, NCG 6118 will go poof and you might not ever find her again."

"How *do* you find her again?" I don't need Lila to explain her fascination with the constellation, her fear of losing it forever. Its austere beauty stirs something cold in my breast.

"I memorized her position. Also, I've got a chart with the coordinates and the Dreyer description. Doesn't make it easy, though."

"You wrote it down? Where?"

"It's in my stuff. In my suitcase."

"I'd love to see it," I say.

"Yeah? Why? This some kind of trick to get me cozy in my trailer?"

I wrestle my gaze from the telescope and take her small hand in mine. "Something like that."

"Man alive, I'd love to see it through a real telescope."

I think about the mega-powerful telescope owned by the Redfield Observatory and tremble. "What about your family? Couldn't your dad pull a few strings?"

"Yeah, if I hadn't left him behind for all this." She laughed. "I haven't spoken to him in…a while."

"Father-daughter relationships are the worst," I say.

We pack it in and meander to her trailer. She shares it with a couple of other girls, but one missed the trip, and the other stays with a boyfriend when she's in town. Nothing happens. We have a couple of Southern Comfort nightcaps. Then she falls asleep on her dumpy couch. After she's snoring, I rummage through her bags and find the astronomical charts she's gathered and stick the one I need into my pocket next to the cold, lethal smoothness of the prod. I smooch Lila's furry cheek on my way out the door.

* * *

The storm broadsides the estate an hour or so before dark.

The Doctor has sent word that I'm to report to the laboratory at once. He requires me at the crank that revs up the dynamo. Like all his gadgets, the crank is unwieldy and impractical and nobody else is physically strong enough to make it turn with sufficient speed. The combination of my efforts and the electrical storm are crucial one-two punches in the pursuit of scientific progress. Tonight's the night he jump starts yet another patchwork corpse, and maybe this time it'll work and he'll snag the Nobel and show his lamentably deceased dad who the *real* scientist is in the family.

At the moment, I'm on the front porch, standing beneath the awning, goggling at nature's wrath. Thin, jagged bolts of lightning splinter in white hot strokes that repeat every fifteen to twenty seconds. Wind and rain crash upon the eaves like an avalanche. By some confluence of atmospheric forces, the air dims and reddens as the grounds have been transmogrified into the soundstage of a Martian epic. I swing my hand back and forth, fascinated at how it seems to float and multiply as it drags through the bloody light. I skip from the sheltering eaves toward the middle of the driveway, feigning carefree abandon as I throw my hands skyward and tilt my face so water streams from it. The reality is, the strikes are marching ever closer and I want to get the hell clear of the house.

Pelt sits in a rocker by the rail of the third floor balcony. He strikes a match on the sole of his cowboy boot and lights one of his nasty hand rolled cigarettes I can smell from a hundred yards away. He eyes me with the cold intensity of a raptor studying a mouse and I wonder if his instincts are actually that damned sharp. Could he really know? The notion chills me in a way the deluge can't.

A second later none of that matters. Lightning flares directly overhead, and I feel in my bones that this is it, *this* bolt has been drawn into the array. And man, oh, man, had I screwed that over big time earlier in the day. I clap my hand over my eyes. The blue-white flash stabs through the cracks between my fingers. The top of the house explodes and the effect is epic beyond my fondest dreams. The concussion sits me down, hard, as all the windows on this side of the building shatter. Fiery chunks of wood, glass, and stone arc upward and outward in a ring. Debris crashes to earth in the gardens, is catapulted among the waving treetops. It's glorious.

The house remains upright, although minus a substantial portion of the third story. Smoke pours down the sides of the building, thick and black, and chivvied by blasts of wind; it roils across the muddy yard and acres of lawn, lowering a hellish, apocalyptic shroud over the works. I'm on my feet again and primed for violence. Pelt will be coming for me. Except, the sly bastard's vanished—his left boot is stuck in the mud near the front steps. I hope against hope he's dead. Servants stumble through the smoke, clutching each other. Their quarters occupy the ground floor, so I doubt any got caught in the explosion. This is their lucky day. None of them glance at me as they file past, moaning and sobbing like a chain of ghosts.

I have to be sure. The rain kills the worst of the flames, snuffs them before they can create an inferno. The grand staircase is in sorry shape. Several steps are gone. I hopscotch my way onward and upward while lightning flashes through the giant hole in the ceiling. Happily, the laboratory, its various sinister machines, have been obliterated. Upon closer inspection, I spy the Doctor's mangled and gruesomely mutilated person fallen through the floor where it lies pinned beneath a shattered beam. His body is burnt and crushed. He's quite mindless in his agonies, shrieking for his dead parents and the friends he doesn't have.

Yeah, I should finish the job. That's the smart move. Alas, alack, I'm too melodramatic to take the easy way out.

* * *

The Doctor keeps a machine in the cellar. When I'm feeling blue I sneak down and bathe in its unearthly glow. It kicks mad scientist-old school; a mass of bulbs and monster transistors, Tesla coils, exposed circuitry, and cables as thick as pythons going every which way. At the heart of this '50s gadgetry is a bubble of glass with an upright table for a passenger. Allegedly the bubble shifts through time and space. Dr. Kob's grandfather built the prototype in 1879, powered it via lightning stored in an array of crude batteries. The new model still runs on deep cycle batteries Dr. Kob Jr. scavenged from backhoes and bulldozers.

The main reason the Master traps lightning to energize his devices is because they suck so much juice the electric bill would draw prying eyes sooner rather than later. There's a backup diesel generator gathering dust for a true emergency. The Doctor is sentimental about his methods, obsessed with the holistic nature of the process. He won't drive or fly, won't operate a computer, not even a typewriter. He scratches in his voluminous journals with quill and ink. In the mansion, every lamp runs on kerosene, the stoves and furnaces, coal, our black and white televisions and radios, batteries. We're like an evil alternate universe version of the Amish.

The T&S machine holds special significance for me, because that's the device of my genesis, my cradle and incubator. Dr. Kob reached back into the great dark heart of prehistory to pluck an egg from my mother's womb and fertilized it with God knows what. He effected a few cosmetic alterations to bring me marginally in line with the latest iteration of the species, dressed me up like a real girl, taught me to walk and talk and hold a spoon. He forbade my partaking in any sort of significant education— apparently he couldn't reconcile his anthropological interest with his fear that I might become too smart for his health. Indeed, I'm certain if he ever had the slightest inkling of my true intellectual capacity, he'd have sent Pelt to slit my throat in the night.

However, I learned to read, no thanks to him. Poor dearly departed Goldilocks took care of that on the sly. I was ripping through college level lit by the tender age of fourteen. Eliza Doolittle, eat your heart out.

The procedure hasn't been without unexpected complications, however. You wouldn't believe my psychedelic dreams, and if I'm ever caught and placed on trial for crimes against humanity, I'll get an insanity pass on the descriptions alone. Genetic memory? I dunno; all I know is that in dreams I go for a ride on an astral carpet to a high desert wasteland that spreads under a wide carnivorous sky. The tribe kills with rocks and clubs; it assembles in caves and lays its feasts upon the dirt. They haven't invented fire, thus meat and skin is crushed and smeared on rocks, like finger paint and wet clay. The brutes, my people, see my apparition, doubtless grotesque in its familiarity, and hoot in alarm and outrage, jam-red mouths agape. Then, the large males, the killers, snarl and snatch up their clubs and their stones, and hop toward me with murder on their minds.

Nine times out of ten, I jerk into wakefulness, alone in my dingy cell with the television screen full of snow. The tenth time out of ten, I come to in a field, naked and covered in scabs of blood, with no memory but the dream memories.

* * *

Even the Doctor isn't quite mad enough to do what I've done. He's a lunatic, yes indeed. He's also a survivor. Better than most, he understands that one screws with the infinite at one's own peril. I'm sure the meticulously recorded results of those Victorian experiments with peasantry cooled his jets.

I, on the other hand, am a desperate sort.

Those nights the good Doctor and his toady spent drunk off their asses, I took the T&S Machine for joyrides. The calibrations weren't difficult—I simply plugged in the various sequences from Doctor Kob's logs. The wild part is, the machine goes forward and back and to any physical location in the universe, provided one has the coordinates. The places I've gone, weirder and more frightening than those Technicolor nightmares.

After Doctor Kob and Pelt murder me in that squalid alley, I give them a moment to wonder at my dying words. But it's only a possible me, a shadow. Travelers exist in duplicate during collocation. It's complicated; suffice to say, each of us unique snowflakes, aren't. We exist as a plurality. That old saw about meeting yourself...it's only kinda true. The universe didn't unravel when I skipped ahead and met one of my future selves, an inveterate alcoholic and aimless wanderer, one bound to run afoul of Dr. Kob's plots of revenge. If she's anything like me (haha!), she won't mind making the sacrifice to even the score.

Pelt knows something's wrong, but even as he turns I tap him with the prod and he's gone in a belch of gas and flame. The Doctor takes it in stride. He's a hobbled shell of a man, yet arrogant as ever. He commands me to drop the weapon and submit to my well-deserved punishment. I slug him and he falls unconscious. That feels so good, I've revisited the moment a dozen times.

This is how it ends for Daddy dearest: I strap him into the machine and send him to the land of my ancestors, and once he's evaporated into the abyss of Time I take an axe to the machine. I've gotten my kicks. That conscience I've been incubating stings like hell. Who knows what havoc I might wreak on material existence were I to keep dicking around with the timestream.

I sent the Doctor with a mint copy of *Frankenstein*, a dozen bottles of wine, and the prod with a full charge. It's the least I could do. The very least.

* * *

I track the Banning Circus to a show in Wenatchee. The owner, the great, great grandson of Ezra Banning, is skeptical when I apply for the strongman job. He's got a strongman, he says, and I say I know. I also know his guy is getting long in the tooth and suffers from asthma, or emphysema, or whatever. Banning tells me to hit the bricks, he's a busy man, blah, blah. I walk over to the lion cage and tear the door off its hinges—naturally, I try to make it look casual, but the effort does me in for the day. The owner picks up his jaw. He sends one of his flunkies to break the news to poor Cleo. He doesn't even mind that it takes Armand the better part of two days and the assistance of local animal control to corral their lion and get him into his cage.

I knock on Lila's trailer door. A monster storm cloud is massing in the north and that could be good or bad. It certainly sets the scene. My hair is standing on end. Lila screams and throws her arms around me. She's crying a little and there's snot in her beard.

"Hey, this is for you," I say and give her a small wooden coffer I bought off a guy at a garage sale where I also scored some dumbbells to get in shape for my strongman—*strongperson*—audition.

"What is it?" She lifts the lid and gasps. An eerie golden light plays over her face.

"Stardust."

"Stardust?"

"I hope it's not radioactive. Maybe we should get a Geiger counter."

"You're yanking my chain."

I smile. "Never happen."

"Well...my God. Look at this. Where...?"

I take the folded, spindled, and mutilated piece of paper with the Dreyer entry for galaxy N1168 from my pocket and give it to her. Lightning parts the red sky like a cleaver. It reflects twin novas in her eyes. I grasp her free hand and press it against my heart.

Three, two, one. Boom.

X'S FOR EYES

Laird Barron

WITHDRAWN

31901059342487

CPSIA information can be obtained
at www.ICGtesting.com
Printed in the USA
FSOW01n0021170516
20441FS